DELIRIUM'S MUSE

Michaël Wertenberg

Contents

WHAT HAPPENED TO MELISSA

The houses on Fairview Lane were a uniform blue Mom called 'sky blue', though it didn't much resemble the blue of the sky. There was more of a greenish tint to it, like lake water. I suggested we call it lake-water blue, but Mom only chuckled. She continued to call it 'sky blue'. It wasn't ugly. I suppose if all the houses had to be the same colour, 'sky blue' was as good a colour as any.

Our house was the second to last on Fairview Lane—perhaps third to last if you count Mr Bleaker's house which stood dead centre at the end of the cul-de-sac, but his house hid behind a large elm whose low-hanging branches obscured all but a corner of the roof from view. And if I can't see it, I don't count it. Fairview Lane was at a steep incline, and from the bottom of the street, our house was on the left.

Mrs Pomeroy lived directly across the street from us in a house that mirrored ours in every way. When I looked at our side of the street from the end of her driveway, I could see that our house was the only one that stood straight. The Prestons lived next door, and their home leaned a bit toward ours, as did Mrs Farlen's house on the other side. The inclination was only slight, but it was noticeable. Sometimes, especially late at night when Fairview Lane was lit only by the star-speckled sky, it appeared that our house was whispering secrets and the neighbouring houses were leaning in slightly to listen. I think that's a fair analogy, as the residents of our little community weren't exactly big on discretion or staying out of other people's business. Mrs Pomeroy was no exception. She'd often comment on what a neighbour had said or done, as if it was any business of hers. I remember one day, I told her it wasn't nice to talk about the neighbours like that, but she said we had to stick together and that being concerned about your neighbours was a good thing.

Just beyond Fairview Lane—supposedly several miles beyond, though I feel 'just' is a better word—stood the Rockies: dark grey rocks, with cracks of white spidering horizontally. They, too, leaned slightly toward our house—well, toward all the houses on Fairview Lane. One street down from us, parallel to us, was Crescent Ridge. It was neither crescent-shaped nor did it sit on a ridge, just like the view from our street was many things but not 'fair'.

The contradictions used to bother me a lot, and I would often comment on them. Mrs Pomeroy suggested I do some research on the names. She even drove me to the Denver library and helped me sift through public records to find out why the streets in our neighbourhood were given the names they were given.

I discovered that Crescent Ridge used to be called Seiderman Way, named after the city planner Justin Seiderman. There was a park named after him, too. Years after he died it came to light that he had molested several young girls, one of whom his daughter. The park that once bore his name is now simply Municipal Park, and Seiderman Way is now Crescent Ridge. That still didn't explain why they chose the name Crescent Ridge, but it did make me more comfortable with the contradiction.

I couldn't find any information on the naming of Fairview Lane, but I suspected City Planner Justin Seiderman had something to do with it.

I was twelve years old, and Melissa, thirteen, when we moved from Boulder to Fairview Lane. Melissa only had one more year before high school, and supposedly Park County had the best high school in the state. Not that high schools in Boulder weren't good—I'm sure they were—but Mom wanted the best for Melissa, and Dad worked hard to provide for that.

Though we could have waited a year before moving, Mom said we were right to come when we did; said I'd have time to adjust. She said it'd be difficult at first, but with time everything would be okay. That was the expression I'd heard over and over again in Boulder: with time everything will be okay. I think saying that, in some way, was how we got through that last year in Boulder, so I didn't bother pointing out all the obvious ways it wasn't true.

We moved in late June: time to get settled in, meet the neighbours, and 'adjust' before the start of school.

Melissa didn't need any time to adjust. She was at ease everywhere she went and in any context she was in. I'm sure I'm exaggerating, but that's the impression I had. She was always smiling and always had a positive, bright thing to say. Her enthusiasm and optimism were contagious. I couldn't help but smile and be happy when I was around my sister. Even though we didn't talk much, she made me happy and she made the move I so dreaded actually a very positive thing—at least positive at first.

Melissa was more eager to meet the neighbours than I was. She saw a group of kids our age hanging out in Finley Square and went right up to them. I didn't. The kids were a bit older than me and a bit older than Melissa, too, but even if they had been my age, I don't think I would have had the nerve.

Finley Square wasn't a square at all (yet another Park County misnomer). Finley Square was a bend in Colorado Avenue, where one could continue on to Denver or turn right up to the collection of cul-de-sacs that formed our little suburb. There was a grocery store, a crafts shop, and a restaurant, and a parking lot that was excessively large for the little commerce it hosted. Mom said that Finley Square looked like a smile welcoming us home. I could see why she said that: the restaurant and grocery store could have been the eyes (though perhaps cross eyed) with their awnings the eyelashes; and the parking lot curved like a wide grin. Cars always parked close to the shops which made the 'smile' look like it was missing its bottom row of teeth. I'd always hope to see it one day with two trucks parked among the cars like the fangs of a vampire, but that never happened. One day a camper was parked in between two cars. That was as close to a blood-sucking beast as I ever saw. Two campers would have been better, but I suppose you really only need one fang to suck blood.

School wouldn't be for another six weeks; Mom actually encouraged Melissa to spend time at Finley Square and get to know the neighbourhood kids. I'd sometimes tag along. But I'd always stay out of her way.

The kids in our new neighbourhood took to Melissa immediately, opened up and accepted her like they were long-time friends. We had only been there a few short weeks and already our backyard porch welcomed the neighbourhood kids on an almost daily basis. Melissa had a North-African drum, a djembé, that our Uncle Teddy had given her. She was quite good at drumming. I had a guitar, though I couldn't really play it. Other kids brought other instruments; most would just sing. And there was music and happiness. At first Mom stayed out of the way. But she couldn't help herself, and when she'd bring out refreshments and snacks, she'd invariably linger and try to join in. She was actually a pretty good singer and knew the words to a lot of the classic rock songs Tommy Preston would play. I didn't know the lyrics to any songs, so I'd just rap my fingers against my glass to the beat and bob my head and smile.

All the other kids took turns beating on Melissa's djembé. I never asked to, and Melissa never offered.

Since my birthday was on July 3rd, my family would usually have a barbecue and a birthday party on the same occasion. For our first July 4th in our new community, we didn't host a barbecue but, instead, went to one on our street. There would be a birthday cake and some presents at home for later.

The barbecue was in Gene and Meryl Stinson's yard, six houses down from us. I suspected nearly the entire neighbourhood was there. With fences only at the front of the houses on Fairview Lane and none separating the backyards, the barbecue inevitably spilled over into Mr Friedman's property, who had his own barbecue set up as well, with, in my opinion, much better burgers.

There were three kids my age: Kevin, Jimmy, and Rachel. Rachel kept with her parents, while Kevin, Jimmy, and I explored the woods and played war by the dried-up creek.

In between battles, we'd retreat to either Mr Friedman's or the Stinsons' for provisions. I'd search the clusters of people and try to spy Melissa. Only once did I see her. She was laughing with a group of grownups, always at ease, with kids and parents alike.

For my 13th birthday, I received a digital camera and a printer with special paper. The following day, I stood at the end of Mrs Pomeroy's driveway and took pictures of the Rockies towering over our street. When I printed the photos, I measured the images. Our house was 2.4 cm tall, and the Rockies 1.8 cm. The jagged mountains seemed far less menacing on paper. They even looked quite beautiful, like you'd see on a post card: Here I am. Wish you were here.

I took more photos the next day, still the same subject: our house with the Rocky Mountains behind, looming over it. My measurements weren't exactly the same: our house 2.37 cm and the Rockies 1.82. I would need to be more exact: more exact in the spot and height where I took the photos from, and more exact with the angle of my camera. I really needed a tripod, but I would have to make do with what I had. I stood at the end of

Mrs Pomeroy's driveway, my left foot over a distinctive V-shaped crack. I stood straight, camera at eye-level. Our house 2.41 cm, the Rockies 1.79 cm. I printed out the photo, dated it, and thumbtacked it to the corkboard in my bedroom. The next day I repeated the process and came up with the same measurements. I thumbtacked that photo next to the other one. I had to move the corkboard to a different wall so I could look at it from my bed at night. It was supposed to be comforting now that I had proof that the mountains weren't growing or gaining on us, but I only had two photos. More would be needed.

One day, Mrs Pomeroy asked me what I was doing there in her driveway with my camera.

I answered with a question of my own. 'Do you feel it, too? Like the Rockies are hovering over our street, threatening to come crashing down on us any day?'

She ruffled my hair and called me a 'curious boy' and said that I had an active imagination. I don't think she meant it to be mean, but I was hurt nonetheless.

By August 1st, I had eleven photos of our house and the Rockies behind it thumbtacked to my corkboard. The measurements were consistent, only the colour of the sky had changed. My favourite photo was from July 16th when the sky was cloudy and the peaks of the Rockies disappeared into the clouds. In that photo, the mountains seemed to be reaching upward and not looking down on our little street.

I made several copies of that photo and filled my corkboard with them. They were meant to keep the bad dreams away, and for a while they did. I should have given one of the photos to Melissa. There were a lot of things I should have done, like put the camera away, hide it in the back of a drawer buried under piles of neatly folded clothes. But Mrs Pomeroy was right, I was a curious boy—overly curious perhaps—with an overly active imagination.

***

I wore dark slacks and a sky-blue button-down shirt for the first day of school. I had breakfast—milk and toast with honey—alone. Apparently, I was far more eager to start school than anyone else. Mom was still asleep and Melissa too—unless she had already left and was waiting at the bus stop. The bus was scheduled to pass at 7:25, and it was only 6:55. I wasn't eager to get to school, but the image of my sister—who was always eager and enthusiastic, even for school— waiting alone at the bus stop motivated me to make an early start of it.

Mrs Pomeroy was standing at the end of her driveway. She asked me if I was sure I didn't want her to drive me. I thanked her and said I was taking the bus. She probably meant well, but she gave me the creeps. She'd always speak slowly and softly like each word hurt her to come out, and she'd always look me straight and deep in the eyes: overly intimate, creepy. I could feel her eyes on me as I walked down Fairview Lane toward the bus stop. I didn't turn around.

It had only been two months, but already I knew her whole life story. The whole neighbourhood knew it. Her husband had died about a year ago: heart attack while taking a shower, slipped, hit his head, and drowned. Drowned in the shower, his own shower! Her only child, a son a year younger than me, ran away shortly thereafter. I'd feel sad for her if she wasn't so creepy, always in my business, 'What are you up to?' 'Where are you going?' Crazy lady. Crazy, sad lady.

Melissa wasn't at the bus stop. No one was. I smiled. I'd tease her and call her slow when she came.

Cindy Fleming and her younger brother, Bobby, arrived before Melissa. She wore a yellow skirt, which was a terrible colour for her. Bobby wore a shirt the same colour as mine. I thought about running home to change, but I couldn't risk missing the bus on my first day.

'Hello,' she said. 'First day of school, already.'

I mumbled 'hello' back. Bobby stared at me with an open mouth. Even when I scowled at him he wouldn't look away. I suspected Bobby would have a lot of problems at school. Thankfully, he was still in grade school and not Junior High like me and Melissa and Cindy.

The bus arrived before Melissa. I asked the bus driver to wait just one more minute. 'My sister is coming. She's right behind me,' I said.

The bus driver looked behind me and shook her head. 'Step in if you want a ride. I'm pulling out.'

Maybe Melissa got a ride from a friend and didn't tell me because there wasn't any room for me in the car. That was the most likely explanation, though it didn't help put me at ease.

I sat in the front seat so I could see the same thing the driver was seeing. I'd also be the first face the kids would see when they stepped on the bus. I made a point of looking them all in the eyes and smiling. I could tell many of them were nervous, but they all smiled back.

Melissa was starting the eighth grade, and me, the seventh. We had no classes together, but I looked for her in the halls. Right before sixth period gym, I saw her and a group of girls standing by some lockers. Melissa was in the centre of the group. She held her books to her chest and smiled and laughed with the other girls. I wasn't aware that I'd been tense—probably just first-day-of-school nerves—but when I saw her smiling and laughing, I felt calm and relieved.

Melissa wasn't on the bus home, either. Though I was dying to know who she'd gotten a ride with, I promised myself I wouldn't ask. Maybe Mom would ask, or if she already knew, maybe she'd let it come out in conversation.

That conversation would have to wait, as Mom wasn't home when I arrived back from school. Neither was Melissa nor Dad for that matter. I looked around making sure the coast was clear before I pulled the spare key from under the welcome mat and let myself in. I had the house to myself, and with no one to welcome me when I entered, I did feel a bit like an intruder. It was kind of exciting.

I tiptoed through the living room. I opened drawers and rummaged through their contents before placing everything back the way I'd found it and wiping away my fingerprints with my shirt sleeve like I'd seen on TV. I fixed myself a baloney sandwich, washed and put away the plate, and got rid of all crumbs and evidence of the sandwich.

Shortly past five, keys jingled at the front door. I ran up the stairs and crouched behind the pillar to the bannister. I had a perfect view of Melissa as she entered, hung up her jacket, and walked across the room to the kitchen. My heart thumped loud in my chest, even though I was sure she wouldn't notice I had been there. And even if she had? Still, it was fun to pretend.

A moment later, Melissa returned to the living room with a can of soda in hand. She sat down on the couch and flipped on the TV. Her on the couch, me in the upstairs hallway peeking over the bannister, together we watched music videos, but Melissa seemed more focused on her phone. She rattled off text after text. Melissa was always so fast at typing on her phone, the fastest I'd ever seen.

I grew bored and wished she'd change the channel. As if reading my mind—apparently, some siblings share this kind of psychic connection— she grabbed the remote and flipped through the channels, found nothing of interest, and shut off the TV. A few text messages later, she got up and returned to the kitchen. It was the perfect opportunity for me to make my getaway.

I was two steps down the stairs when the front door opened. Mom! I quickly back peddled up the stairs.

'Hello, I'm home,' she called out.

Neither Melissa nor I answered.

Mom sighed and closed the door with her foot while she clutched the overstuffed paper bag of groceries. I tried to peek inside the bag from my lofty vantage point, but the groceries were covered with a celebrity magazine. She disappeared into the kitchen where I heard her talk to Melissa.

'How was school, honey?'

'It was fine, Mom. I have three classes with Stacey.'

Who is Stacey? I made a mental note.

'I got Mr Wilhelm for History.'

'Is that good or bad?' Mom asked.

It was bad. Everybody knew that. Mr Wilhelm was the toughest teacher and assigned loads of homework.

I couldn't hear much of the conversation through the rustling of the paper bag and cupboards being opened and shut, but I did make out that Mom was going to cook hamburgers for dinner. I was glad. I loved hamburgers, and Mom made the best ones.

My heart raced as footsteps left the kitchen but did not return to the couch. I saw only the top of Melissa's head, but I could tell she was coming toward the stairs. I managed to skip down the hallway, out the window, and onto the ledge before she could see me. Close call!

I wanted to peek in from outside, but it was too risky. Instead, I held my breath, sucked in my tummy, and listened to her pass. Behind the stone wall to my right was Melissa's room. Her window was much more difficult to reach, but not impossible. I saw her light come on. If she had just opened her window and stuck her head out, she would have seen me standing on the back ledge. And wouldn't that have been a strange thing to explain?

I stood straight and still, waited, and listened. The cackle of a few birds high in the trees were my only company until Melissa turned on some music in her room. I didn't know who the singer was, but I quite liked it. I made a mental note to ask Melissa later who the singer was.

I had been standing on the ledge for what seemed like hours, though I didn't have my timer with me to be exact. My legs ached, but I had trained for such an occasion and my legs did not buckle. I resisted the urge to scale down the drainage pipe. It ran just by the kitchen window, and I couldn't chance Mom spotting me. It's no fun if you get caught.

The wind picked up, and I was not dressed for standing outside on the ledge. But I had to be patient and wait for the right time to get down.

A car pulled in the driveway. I couldn't see it, but it was surely Dad, which meant that it must have been around 6:30 pm. The car door slammed shut, which made me jump. I nearly fell off the ledge.

We always had dinner right when Dad got home, so I waited a few more minutes before climbing down the drainage pipe. I should have gone down head first to peek so that I could look into the kitchen and make sure no one could see me. *I'll have to train for that.* I made a mental note.

Predictably, my family was in the dining room adjacent to the kitchen, and I made it to the ground unseen. I walked to the brush that bordered the woods in the backyard and lay, stomach flat, on the ground. The brush was good for hiding, but it was farther away from the window than I would have preferred. It wasn't a perfect view of my family, either—Melissa was seated with her back to me—but I got a good look at Dad and saw that he was happy and talking with joy to the two women he loved.

The next morning, I woke up extra early so I could take a photo without Mrs Pomeroy peeking out from between the curtains and catching me on her driveway. Our house 2.41 cm, the Rockies 1.79 cm: the same as in the afternoon. (You can never be too careful.)

***

Mrs Pomeroy was weird again today. She was at her driveway when I walked to the bus stop. She handed me a brown paper bag with a banana and an orange. I took it and said 'thank you'. Mom would have wanted me to be polite, though I don't know how she would have reacted to a neighbour giving me fruit, again.

I felt her eyes on me all the way down the street. Cindy and Bobby

Fleming were waiting when I arrived. They were always at the bus stop before me, except on Mondays. I wondered why that was, but I couldn't find a good way to ask so I kept silent. (I never did find out why they were always late on Mondays.)

I made friends quickly. Unsurprising. I was Melissa's brother. Everyone wanted to be close to Melissa. Jimmy Spears was no exception. He was always on the bus in the front seat waiting for me. He'd talk about other things, baseball mostly, but I knew where his mind really was; I'd seen the way he looked at her. I couldn't fault him; it's gross, she's my sister and all, but as long as Jimmy didn't say anything about it and just looked, I couldn't get too mad.

At least Jimmy wasn't like Neil O'Brien, who I quickly learned to avoid. Neil was always talking about girls, and it didn't matter to him that Melissa was my sister. He once said to me that she should wear tighter shirts. I nearly went off and clocked him right there, but we were seated in English class. He actually had to leave early for a band concert—good for him, because I still wanted to clock him after class, and I would have, too.

Now, I just ignore him.

My teachers were all great. Two of them, Mrs Baleroy and Mr Pix, I shared with Melissa—though in different classes of course. I wasn't exactly the best student in Boulder, but I felt things were going to be different here. For the first time in a long time, I actually enjoyed going to school and even looked forward each Sunday to the coming week. The only thing I dreaded, actually, was coming home from school Monday afternoon. Monday was picture day.

For the second weekend in September, Billy Wagner threw a back-to-school party. He didn't invite me. Why would he? Billy was a junior in high school. But I heard about the party from his brother, Ethan, who was in second period math with me.

I didn't know who Melissa had heard about the party from. I didn't even know she was going. But I saw her leave the house with Cynthia Stansing, so I followed them. I walked on the other side of the street at a distance. It didn't matter; they never turned around or looked over their shoulders. They walked down Fairview Lane, across Wicks, and down Crescent Ridge, talking really loud. I couldn't make out any of their conversation, just that there was excitement in their voices and in their steps as well—I had to walk at a quick pace to keep up.

Billy Wagner lived at the bottom of Crescent Ridge. Still, I expected Melissa and Cynthia to keep walking past the house, maybe down to Finley Square. But they didn't. They turned and went right inside Billy Wagner's house. I didn't think Mom would have let Melissa go to a high school party, but Melissa never lied to Mom or kept anything from her so I didn't know what to think. It was all quite confusing, and it didn't make me feel good.

I stopped two houses shy of the party. I could hear voices and music spilling into the street. The voices sounded older, like high schoolers' voices, and the music didn't sound like anything Melissa ever listened to. No, I was not feeling very good at all.

I walked to the far side of the house where a row of thick, tall elms separated the house from the backs of the shops on Finley Square. I didn't have my timer with me, so I did it in my head: twenty-eight seconds to get to the fourth bough. I could have done it much faster, but the first bough was so hard to reach. The vantage point was not nearly as good as I'd expected. In fact, the only window I could see into was angled, and I only saw a bookshelf and the occasional elbow or back of someone's head. It would have been a good vantage point if I wanted to assassinate a target. But I didn't even have a slingshot with me, much less a rifle with a scope.

I heard voices coming from outside the house, in the backyard— three voices, perhaps four with one not having much to say. I waited and watched for them to step into view, but they never did. I did see something bright and cross-shaped whiz through the air and smack into a tree. It made a 'pop'—like when you flip your thumb from the corner of your mouth—then shattered, and the voices hooted and hollered.

It was only then that my wrist started to hurt from when I'd twisted it in the climb. I didn't think it was anything at the time—a ninja knows how to ignore pain—but after probably an hour in the tree, it was stiff and sore. I wondered, if I had broken my wrist and couldn't get back down, like a scared cat, who would find me, and what would I tell them? I didn't think anyone would be able to find me, not if I didn't let them. I'd stay in the tree until my wrist healed, then I'd climb down on my own. And I wouldn't tell anybody anything. I would get real hungry in the tree, waiting for my wrist to heal, but a ninja also knows how to ignore hunger.

I learned a lot about Cynthia Stansing in the following weeks. She was only an eighth grader, but she'd already had two boyfriends, not at the same time, though I think they were friends, or at least on the football team together, and they were both in high school. She wasn't a very good student. She once painted a picture of the school getting eaten by a giant frog for art class, and last year she got real sick and had to miss five months of school.

She didn't seem like a good friend for Melissa. It wasn't like me to think bad things about Melissa's friends. But in a new school, it's important—very important—to get off to a good start. Even in Park County, you can get labelled real quickly, then trying to shake that label can be next to impossible. Like Mrs Pomeroy, for example: she would always be the lady whose husband died in his own shower and whose son ran away. It didn't help that she was spacey and creepy. Even if she weren't, she'd still never be able to shake that label.

Melissa needed to get out of her metaphoric Cynthia shower before she slipped and got stuck with a label she wouldn't be able to shake.

***

October in Colorado can be a strange month. We expect the cold and dress accordingly, but a burst of sun can fool us into thinking summer has returned and allow us a day to live out that fantasy. Our first October Sunday on Fairview Lane was one such day. Dad promptly got out the barbecue. Mom and Melissa spread word throughout the neighbourhood, and by two o'clock we had nearly thirty people in our backyard eating, drinking, talking, and playing.

I let the other kids play my guitar while I sat back and watched and listened. Cynthia Stansing was at Melissa's side the whole time. I noticed something different about Melissa that day and suspected it was related to her being around Cynthia. Melissa, who never wore make up—not that Mom forbade it, it just wasn't Melissa's style—had streaks of dark eyeliner on her eyelids that curved upward into points. She also had her nails painted black. It didn't exactly look bad on her, it just didn't look like Melissa. I saw Mom catch a glimpse of her nails and saw some concern in her expression, though she didn't say anything, at least not in front of me.

Melissa sat quietly for the most part. She let other kids play her drum, and she didn't sing much even when someone played a song I knew she knew the lyrics to.

The food was delicious, I'll admit, but I had no appetite. Something wasn't right. A barbecue in October is unnatural, and by five o'clock the illusion of summer had given way to reality. Melissa wrapped herself in Mom's shawl, but she still shivered. Dad was wearing shorts, but I could see the gooseflesh on his legs, and I knew that he, too, was uncomfortable.

By seven o'clock all the guests had left except Jimmy Spears. He wanted to help clean up—or so he said—but I suggested we go into the woods to play, and he agreed.

I didn't have anything against Jimmy, not really, but I didn't understand why we were friends. We had very little in common. He liked to splash in the creek and throw rocks at bushes and trees. He was a terrible ninja, the opposite of stealth.

While he skipped rocks in the creek, I cleared out a bit of brush and made a secret lair that I could crawl into and hide. Through the branches, I could see Mom and Melissa cleaning up while Dad packed up the barbecue. It would be at least eight months till he'd be able to pull it out again, and even from the distance I was at, I could see the sadness in his eyes.

'What are you doing?' asked Jimmy.

'Watching,' I said.

'You need binoculars.'

'Infra-red binoculars!' I exclaimed.

'Pete Hollbrock has infra-red binoculars and an infra-red shotgun,' said Jimmy. 'His brother's in the military and gets him all kinds of neat stuff. He showed me his gun once.'

Pete Hollbrock was a freshman who lived next to Jimmy. I hated Pete. He was a bully, though he never bullied me.

'Where does he keep his binoculars?' I asked.

'I dunno. Why do you ask?'

I asked because Jimmy was right, I needed binoculars, and Pete didn't deserve them. 'You live next door to him. You could creep into his room and take them. I bet he has them out on his desk or a shelf or something.'

'What? You're crazy. I'm not breaking into Pete Hollbrock's room.'

Jimmy Spears was a terrible ninja and a scaredy cat. I told him I had homework to do, so we walked back to his house then I went back to mine.

On Wednesday, Melissa had her nails painted light grey and she wore matching mascara. I saw her before sixth period gym talking to a couple of boys, and she twirled a lock of hair in her index finger. I'd seen a lady do that on TV recently, though I forget what show, but I'd never seen Melissa do that before. It didn't look right. The grey nails didn't look right either. I wondered how many days she could wear make-up before Mom intervened.

The following Wednesday made it eleven days in a row Melissa wore make-up, always grey or black and never too much. Coach Ritz said he'd send me to the principal's office if I was late to gym one more time, so I only got a glimpse of who Melissa was talking to and I didn't have time to see if she was still twirling her hair.

I was feeling particularly anxious on the bus ride home. I didn't know what it was, exactly, but I knew something wasn't right. The feeling grew as I walked up Fairview Lane. I stopped at Mrs Pomeroy's driveway and looked down in disbelief. It had been repaved! My V-shape crack was gone, and I'd have to start all over with my pictures. It was my fault; I hadn't been meticulous enough. I should have used a tape measure instead of something so arbitrary and fleeting as a crack in the pavement. I was angry with myself and angry with Mrs Pomeroy. Her driveway was fine! Why did she need to repave it?

I tore down all the photos from my corkboard and ripped them all up into tiny pieces. I peeked out my window at the Rockies. They had encroached again; I was sure of it. But my research was ruined, and I had no proof. I made a mental list: tape measure, a tripod, and infra-red binoculars.

Christmas was eight weeks away. I could ask for those things, but could I wait that long? What danger was I running by leaving the Rockies unchecked? I put my concerns aside and somehow managed to get some sleep. When I woke the next day, all was terribly wrong.

Mrs Pomeroy was extra creepy that morning. She handed me a brown paper bag with a banana, an orange, and a peanut butter and jelly sandwich. She told me not to get into trouble at school, like it was any business of hers! She even ruffled my hair and patted my head like I was some sort of a pet. I tried to be nice to her. Her husband had died and her son had run away. I knew she must have been very sad, but I was worried what Mom or Dad would think if they saw the attention she showed me.

That day though, the Rockies were much taller than they had ever been, and in my desperation, I swallowed my disgust and asked Mrs Pomeroy for help.

'Mrs Pomeroy,' I said as I took the brown bag from her, 'I'd like to take photos, precise photos, but I need a tape measure and a tripod.'

She looked very sad, sadder than usual. She stared off into the distance and did not respond. She nodded her head slowly, and her eyes glazed over with moisture.

'Mrs Pomeroy, do you have a tape measure and a tripod I could borrow?'

She covered her face with her hands and turned to walk back to her house, but not before I could see her cry. Extra creepy.

I gave the brown paper bag to Bobby Fleming at the bus stop. He didn't say 'thank you'. He never said 'thank you'. In fact, I don't believe I ever heard him say anything at all.

I saw Melissa in the halls, just before fourth period history. I stopped dead in my tracks. She wore black nail polish and black eyeliner, and she leaned against a locker talking to a boy, Frankie Stevenson, twirling a lock of hair in her index finger. It wasn't the fact she was talking to Frankie Stevenson that made me freeze, blink, and pinch myself—I'd seen her talk to Frankie before, and Frankie was all right; he didn't bother me. It was the lock of hair she was twirling. It was dyed jet black. Melissa had beautiful sandy-blond hair just like Mom's, just like mine. She didn't look right in black, yet she'd been wearing it more and more frequently. And now the streak in her hair! I wondered what Mom would say. Had she seen it? I hadn't, but now that I thought about it, she had been wearing a beanie recently. I hadn't suspected anything. Why would I? But it was starting to make sense, in a non-sensical kind of way.

After school, I sat on the curb in front of our house and waited for Melissa. I saw Mrs Pomeroy watching me from behind the curtains of her living room. I pretended not to see her, and I sat and waited.

Melissa came home with her now good friend, Cynthia Stansing, who smiled at me. But I didn't smile back.

'Hi, Melissa. What's up with the hair?'

She scowled at me in a way Melissa had never done before. 'You don't like it?'

I shrugged and looked away. 'I thought it was fine before,' I mumbled.

'Are you and Jimmy going to play in the woods?' she asked.

'I suppose.' I looked at Melissa then at Cynthia. 'And you guys?'

Melissa smiled. 'Oh, you know. Girl stuff.'

They went inside, and I saw Jimmy Spears walk up Fairview Lane toward me. I bolted around the house into the woods and into my hiding spot in the brush. I had taken a cushion from the couch and left it there to lie on, but now it was wet and mouldy and smelled bad. *I'll have to get a new cushion.* I made a mental note.

I watched the house. The girls were downstairs in the kitchen where I couldn't see until they cut through the dining room on the way to the stairs. A moment later they reappeared in the upstairs hallway, briefly, before going into Melissa's room. I really needed binoculars. Though it wouldn't have mattered; Melissa closed the blinds of her bedroom window. I didn't even know she had blinds; it was the first time I'd seen them. Surveillance was getting to be more and more difficult.

I chewed on my bottom lip and thought of a plan. I heard Jimmy walking noisily through the woods, kicking at leaves and slapping at tree branches with a stick. He called my name several times, but I didn't answer. He walked right past me without seeing. I crawled out of hiding, on my stomach, then jumped up and grabbed him. He screamed like a little girl. It was very funny. We laughed, and out of the corner of my eye, I saw Melissa at her window, blinds open, looking out for the source of the scream.

'Shhh,' I said, and I pushed Jimmy behind a tree.

'What?' he said, and not with a whisper, despite my clear indications to do so.

I crouched and pointed to Melissa's window.

'Oh,' said Jimmy, and he crouched beside me. 'We need binoculars.'

'I know,' I whispered. 'Tonight we're stealing Pete Hollbrock's binoculars. I have a plan.'

'No way. He'll kill us.'

I smirked. Jimmy was such a wuss.

'He's killed before, you know,' said Jimmy with a straight face.

'No he hasn't. Don't be stupid.'

'I'm not being stupid,' said Jimmy. 'You're being stupid, talking about stealing from Pete Hollbrock.'

'Don't be such a wuss. We're stealing his binoculars and a tripod if he has one.'

'What do we need a tripod for?'

'Don't worry about it. We'll meet under the elm in your backyard at one am.'

'I don't know.'

Jimmy was making me angry. I pushed him down and ran away. 'One o'clock,' I called back. 'Be there.'

Jimmy Spears was a wuss and a terrible ninja, but he'd do just about anything I told him to. I was waiting behind the elm in his backyard at five till one when he came tiptoeing out the back door.

'This is a terrible idea,' Jimmy whispered.

'Shh.' I pointed to the left. 'That's Pete's room with the light on, isn't it?'

Jimmy nodded.

'Excellent.'

Pete Hollbrock's house was smaller than the other houses on the street. There was no drainage pipe that I could scale, but it didn't matter. A large elm with many branches leaned over the house in such a way that even a so-so ninja could climb it, jump on the roof, and crawl down to Pete's window. For me, I could have done it blindfolded.

'You see that tree?'

Jimmy nodded.

'I'm going to climb it. I'll get to his window easily.'

'And then what?'

'That's where you come in.' I could see that I had his attention. 'I need you to create a diversion.'

'Like what?'

'Anything. You just need to make sure he's out of his room. I'll need two minutes, nothing more.'

'How am I supposed to do that?'

Jimmy was not very bright. I was getting angry again.

'I don't know. Why don't you call him?'

'At one o'clock in the morning! And say what?'

I breathed in real deep. I had been training to keep calm in exactly these kinds of situations. Jimmy was, if not much else, at least a good test of my progress. 'Why don't you tell him that there's a prowler in the backyard. You heard him and saw him from your room, and now you see him around his house.'

Jimmy looked scared. 'I don't know.'

'Come on, Jimmy! That's the easy part. You get him outside, even walk around the yard or the woods with him. All I need is two minutes.'

'I don't have my phone.'

I punched him in the arm and pointed to his house. 'Go. Now.'

Jimmy hung his head and sulked back home, and I tiptoed through the shadows over to the elm in Pete Hollbrock's backyard.

I was high up in the tree and had crawled across the bough that dangled above the roof. It was much farther from the roof than it had appeared from the ground. I was going to make a big noise when I landed. I saw Jimmy walk out the back door. He looked around nervously. Then I heard Pete's front door shut, and a moment later Pete, shotgun in hand, was walking toward Jimmy.

Jimmy pointed to the woods between his backyard and Pete's. 'I saw him duck into the woods.'

They walked toward the woods, their feet crunching on dead leaves.

I jumped.

When I landed, it wasn't one big noise that I made but several big noises. I bounced, twisted my ankle, and slammed my knee against the roof. It hurt real bad, but I didn't yell or cry. I lay on my back, holding my ankle, and listened. There wasn't much moonlight to see by, and I couldn't tell where Jimmy had led Pete. I couldn't suppose he had led him out of view—that would have been too clever for Jimmy.

'Where you at?' I heard Pete yell and cock his gun. 'Come out of there, you bastard.' His voice became more distant until it sounded as if it came from Jimmy's part of the woods. I rolled down to the edge of the roof. Pete's window was half opened. This was going to be easy, even with a busted ankle.

I held on to the gutter and swung down to the window sill, opened the window with one hand, and jumped inside.

Pete's room was a disgusting pigsty: dirty clothes scattered everywhere and dirty plates piled on his desk and on the floor. I didn't see any binoculars. I opened the closet: jam-packed with disorder. There might have been a dozen binoculars in there, but I didn't have time to rummage through the mess. Under his bed were two large drawers. I opened the first. Eureka. Binoculars, daggers, nunchucks, throwing stars. I grabbed the binoculars—they were sleek black, light weight, and beautiful—strapped them around my neck, and peeked out the window.

Both Jimmy and Pete were standing under the elm in perfect view of the window. *Geez, Jimmy. You are useless.*

Pete held his shotgun at the ready and turned slowly in a circle. *Should I make a run for the front door? Are his parents up? Or his brother? That would be the worst.*

I started for the door when I heard footsteps in the hallway. They weren't coming in my direction. Another glance out the window showed Jimmy and Pete hadn't left. *Come on, Jimmy. Get him to the other side of the house!*

A voice sounded from down the hall: Pete's father on the telephone. I heard him give his address and say something about a prowler. I presumed he was talking to the police.

A good ninja doesn't panic. I remembered my training and, standing flush against the wall, I concentrated on my breathing. Forty-six breaths later, I heard Pete's voice. He was talking to his father downstairs. Without looking first, I threw open the window and crawled onto the sill. I needed to jump to grab onto the gutter. It was the most dangerous thing I'd ever done, but I did it. I grabbed onto the gutter and pulled myself up onto the roof.

The branch I'd jumped from looked so far away. Even if I jumped with all my might, I wasn't sure I'd be able to reach it. I took a running start. My ankle hurt, but a good ninja pays no mind to the pain. I ran and leapt, and to my surprise, my hands caught the elm's thick branch. I swung and pulled myself onto the branch and scooted down until I could wrap my arms around the trunk. I wish I'd had the foresight to time the whole thing. I was definitely inside Pete's room for more than two minutes, but I bet I executed the daring escape in under ten seconds. Hard to tell for sure, since I hadn't timed it officially.

I was in no hurry to get down. In fact, I climbed farther up the elm, almost to its tippy top where I hid inside a web of small branches. I hugged the trunk, which was much thinner up where I was, and the tree swayed with the breeze. I heard voices below, but there was little light to see. I tried out my brand new infra-red binoculars. Wow! I could see everything: tiny Jimmy Spears, mean Pete Hollbrock with a shotgun and glowing cat-like eyes, and a police officer and someone I assumed was Mr Hollbrock, all in light greens and bright yellows.

I don't know how long I stayed in the tree—at least an hour. I waited till everyone had left and Pete had turned off the light in his bedroom before I climbed down. I wondered when Pete would notice his binoculars were missing and if he'd make the connection with the prowler or with Jimmy Spears. I had to hope he wouldn't. Jimmy Spears was a lot of things, but a good liar was not one of them.

***

It didn't take long for the prowler of Willow Street to turn into an axe-wielding maniac escaped from the madhouse. Jimmy went as far as to say he'd been attacked but managed to fight him off. I suspected most of the embellishments had come from Pete and not from Jimmy. Jimmy just played along. He wasn't much of a story-teller unless a homerun was involved, and 'axe-wielding maniac' seemed more like a Pete Hollbrock invention anyway.

A few weeks later, the prowler was seen on Fairview Lane—that was inevitable—and the police were called out once again. Mom was real shook up. I don't know what she said to the officer, but I saw her from afar and, with my infra-red binoculars, I saw the fear and the worry on her face clear as day. I told her later that I was keeping a look-out and she didn't need to worry. She told me I was a sweet boy and patted me on the head.

I wasn't the only one to volunteer as a look-out. Mr Peterson, Mr Hamlin, Mr Foggart, Mr Bracks, Dad—soon we had a real, organized neighbourhood watch going on. I did most of my watching from the woods, while the neighbours, from other places I could not see.

For five straight nights, Melissa kept her blinds drawn, even though Cynthia Stansing didn't come over. I heard no music coming from her room like before, yet I knew she was there. I could see the light pierce the cracks in the blinds. I didn't think it was healthy for her to be shut in her room with the blinds drawn. I suppose I could have waited to talk to her about that tomorrow at school. But I didn't. I found a smooth pebble and chucked it up to her window. It hit the glass with a light tap and fell back into the darkness where I couldn't see it land. Two minutes later, I repeated with an equally smooth pebble, and two minutes thereafter again until Melissa finally poked her fingers in between the blinds and made a breach to peer out from.

I didn't need the infra-red binoculars to see, since her bedroom light was on. She reminded me of Mom's face from last week, full of worry with untrusting eyes. All of her hair was black, and that was not a trick of the light. She had dyed it the same colour as her nails and mascara. I felt bad for throwing the pebble against her window. I could see that it made her worry, and seeing her like that made me worry too.

For the rest of November, the whole neighbourhood kept watch and the prowler was not seen again. Jimmy stopped coming round, and he sat at the back of the bus with Steve Idle and Craig Winstill. Pete never made a fuss about his missing binoculars—at least not to Jimmy or me. Melissa was spending more and more time alone in her bedroom while I continued to take pictures of the Rockies.

Though I still had no tripod and I knew my measurements were not exact, I was relatively confident that the great towering rock behind us had stopped encroaching on our fair little street. It was during this tenuous period of calm and quiet that the first Christmas decorations began popping up in our neighbourhood. A wreath on a door here, a string of coloured lights hung from a rooftop there—Christmas ornaments came before the first tardy Colorado snowfall. People dressed in red and green and wore a cheerful smile. I anxiously awaited the snow, but it was too warm for snow, too warm for December, and too warm for Christmas decorations, yet nobody seemed to pay that any mind.

I walked home from Finley Square, and Mrs Pomeroy was standing in the middle of the street like she was lost. 'Where have you been?' she asked, though she wasn't looking me in the eye and I didn't know if she was asking about me or her runaway son.

I wasn't comfortable with either possibility, so I found it best to change the subject. I said that Christmas was coming and asked her if she thought it was normal, such warm weather in December. She answered me as if in a daze, 'There's no accounting for the whims of nature.' Then, like when a hypnotist snaps his fingers, she blinked, flashed a forced smile, and added, 'It's good to see you so eager for Christmas.'

Truth be told, I was eager for Christmas, eager for a break in school. Kevin Kramer was really working my nerves. He was a stupid, mean kid who thought he was funnier than he was—which was not at all funny. He called me 'Pom-pom' and laughed. I hated that nickname, so I punched him in the arm. He didn't punch me back. Kevin Kramer wasn't that stupid.

***

Billy Wagner was going to throw another party: one of his famous winter-break parties. Everyone at school was talking about it, even the seventh graders. I wasn't invited, but neither was Sandy Moeira nor Steve Idle, yet they said they were going anyway. Apparently, it was a kind of open-door party, and everyone was invited, unofficially.

Cynthia Stansing came over at 8 o'clock, and she and Melissa left shortly thereafter.

I followed.

Of course we didn't walk together; I didn't want to embarrass them, and I definitely didn't want to talk to Cynthia Stansing. I kept my distance, and again they never turned or looked over their shoulders to see me.

After they entered Billy Wagner's house, I walked around the block then made my approach. The front door was closed, so I knocked. Nobody answered. Goth music and the sound of many competing conversations troubled me, but I did not turn away.

I rang the doorbell. Nobody came.

Finally, some other kids arrived from down the street; they must have been at least seventeen years old. They looked me up and down and smirked. One of them asked me if I was lost.

'I'm here for Billy Wagner's party,' I said.

They laughed.

'Go home, kid,' said one boy whose face was hidden behind a veil of greasy hair. He opened the door, and the three of them entered the noisy and dimly lit house.

It looked and sounded just like the sort of party Mom wouldn't have wanted us to go to. Surely Billy Wagner's parents weren't there, and I suspected there was alcohol.

I did not go home. Instead, I walked around the house to the back. The house, just like ours, had tall, wide windows that started at my chin and were bordered with drooping vines. I stood against the wall, my head hidden in the vines, inches from the glass. Inside, there were only two table lamps—no overhead lights—but I could see everything clearly.

I couldn't spot Melissa, but a group of teenagers were on the couch drinking from red plastic cups. Another group stood near the stereo, not really dancing, but bobbing and swaying. The music was a terrible dark drone with unintelligible murmurs trying to pass for a melody. People passed in and out of the room. They almost always carried red plastic cups. Aside from the group on the couch, they all seemed as in a haze, not really connecting or even trying to connect with one another.

Perhaps it was the music—though I suspect that was only a small part—but I was overcome with dread and unease. I had to find Melissa and get her out of there. I crept along the stone exterior to the far side of the house—the part that was exposed to the Rockies, where they cut the black veil of the night sky with their jagged edges and leaned in to have a look.

Voices, whispers, and giggles drifted toward me from the backyard. I crouched and glanced in that direction. I saw the flame of a lighter then the ember of a cigarette. I tiptoed around one of the house's protruding rooms to where the cigarette ember was out of sight, to where I was out of sight, hidden between the house and a row of bushes. In front of me was the kitchen. I could spy the tops of cupboards, interrupted by the stove's ventilation shaft like a chimney suspended from the ceiling.

The kitchen window was higher than the other windows and did not grant me easy access. But exactly like our house, beside the window was a thick drainage pipe with wide fastenings running from the ground to the roof every three feet or so. I had climbed ours several times with ease, and this one was no different—though the fastenings were smaller and my shoes scraped the pipe to find a foothold, producing more sound than I had wanted. A small ledge where the kitchen wing joined the rest of the house offered me a place to stand, and much like our house, it hung below the window of the upstairs hallway. There were no lights on upstairs, but enough light from below spilled into the hallway that I could make out three doors, all closed, and the beginnings of a winding staircase.

The window wasn't open—not exactly—but it wasn't properly closed either. With a bit of jiggling and my own house key slipped between the frame and the panes, I was able to flip the tiny latch, pull open the window, and hop inside. I closed the window behind me and felt a sort of claustrophobia sweep over me: the strong sensation of being trapped and suffocating in the smoke- and sweat-filled inside air.

The music changed abruptly to an aggressive thrashing of guitars and deep, guttural singing. I wanted to flee. I wanted to throw open the window and jump to the ground to run away into the woods. But I had to find Melissa. I didn't know what I would say to her or how she would react. *Would she be upset to see me? Or is she now having similar anxieties and would be happy for an excuse to leave?*

I crept along the dark hallway toward the stairs. The floor creaked loudly beneath my feet, but the sound was lost in the chaos of noise coming from below.

From the staircase, I had no view of the ground floor. I had to blindly take it and follow its turn, exposed and unsure of what awaited me. I was not brave. I only acted on a focused need: find Melissa, make sure she's all right. Nothing else guided my steps or regulated my pounding heart. Even when I had made the turn of the stairs and saw below the three kids that had dismissed me at the front door, I did not hesitate. They held red plastic cups and shouted at one another, even though they were huddled together. I stepped around them. The tallest of the three, with brown hair and a thin, brown moustache, saw me, smirked, and went back to his conversation.

I stepped into a sort of living room, though all the furniture, save a couch, had been pushed against the walls. To my left, a group was thrashing to the music. The group was much larger than when I had seen them through the window, and the floor beneath me shook with the thumping of their feet. I saw no sign of Melissa and would have to walk through the group to gain the other room.

As I approached, out of the corner of my eye, I spied an abandoned red plastic cup leaning precariously against the wall from atop the backrest of a chair. I grabbed it and used it to hide my face as I ploughed through flailing limbs and thrashing hair. Fortunately, my cup was empty or I would have been covered in its contents. Peter Stinge slammed into me, then Brady Johnson, then several others I didn't know.

I pinballed my way through and made it to the threshold of another room, smaller, also with chairs pushed back against the walls.

I saw Melissa standing with a boy on the other side of the room. I didn't know who the boy was, and there wasn't enough light for me to get a good look at his face. He wore black, like his hair, and one fingerless glove on his right hand. Melissa wasn't holding a red plastic cup, and I did feel a slight sense of relief. I did not move, but I watched as the boy talked and Melissa smiled and nodded her head. Occasionally, he'd run his gloved hand through his hair, momentarily letting me see his ugly, pale face before his greasy black hair would fall back in place and cover his eyes.

There was plenty of space to go from one room to the other, but most of the kids went out of their way to bump, or elbow, or knock into me as they passed.

I scrunched the red plastic cup in my closed fist and continued to watch. I waited for Melissa to turn and see me, and for this reason I didn't let the anger show on my face. I was good at not letting my emotions show. I'd always practiced this as far back as I can remember. I could hold my hand over a flame for twenty seconds while staring at a mirror and not so much as blink. I could stand in a bucket of ice— that one was more difficult, but with training I could do it and remain poker-faced for well over a minute.

My training was paying off here in the field. The loud, aggressive music, the constant shoulder or elbow knocking me in passing, and the sick stench of smoke wafting towards me from all sides had no effect on me. Eventually, the greaseball stopped talking and took a sip from his red plastic cup. Melissa glanced in my direction. Our eyes met, I'm sure of it, yet she made no sign of surprise or even recognition.

Before I could decide what to say, before I could tell my feet where to carry me, another two boys joined Melissa and the greaseball. Panic gave way to a plan, one that unfolded in my mind with such clarity and precision I knew it could not fail. I turned, dropped my head, and pushed my way through the mosh and into the kitchen. A couple of girls I didn't know were pouring drinks and chatting. I made a bee-line for the sink and began washing my hands. I didn't have to wash for long before the girls left and I was alone.

I took a half-filled bottle of vodka from the counter and splashed the walls and the floor. Though I was terrified someone would come in and catch me, I must admit, it was a lot of fun. With the one lit candle on the table, I lit the other three and spread them out along the counter and left the larger one on the table. I went to the stove-top and opened all six gas rings. The hiss of seeping gas quickly blended with the grunge of music coming from the next room. I knocked the candle to the floor as I exited. The flame did not catch the streaks of vodka like I had hoped, but I knew that was soon to come.

I rushed back to Melissa. I had to make sure she was still there and not on her way to the kitchen. The music was louder and the mosh thicker, and it trapped me in its thrashing and flailing. I fought off the slams. I covered my head with my hands and bulled past a spastic dancer only to find myself again next to the open kitchen door. I listened for the hiss of gas—it was so loud! I watched for flames to spread along the floor and up the walls. I thought I could see the flicker of the candle on the floor, but that might have been my imagination.

I returned to the mosh and felt my way along the outer circle and eventually spilled out on the other side of the room. A group of kids stood at the threshold blocking my passage.

'Excuse me,' I said, and I nudged.

Some kid two heads taller than me and with breath like paint remover mumbled incoherently, his spittle spraying my face. Then he turned his back to me, and I tried again to squeeze through. This time, he grabbed me by the shirt, twisted, and lifted me up and pinned me to the wall. His eyes were red and glazed, his teeth yellow and gritted. Just as he was about to speak, a loud *pop* sounded from behind us. It wasn't the ear-shattering explosion I was expecting, but it carried with it the same result: a loud scream followed by shouts of 'Fire! Fire!' 'Everybody out!'

The kid let me go, and though I badly wanted to stay and watch the flames grow and consume, I spied an open path to the front door and I took it. I was swallowed up in a stream of kids running for the front door, screaming and pushing. I saw Melissa a few heads in front of me. There was no sign of the greaseball who'd been chatting her up. Maybe he wanted to play the hero and had gone to the kitchen to have his greasy head ignited in a grease ball of fire. I couldn't go back to check, though. I was pushed and propelled forward and out the front door.

From the other side of the street, I watched people running out and others running into the house. I saw the smoke billowing in the night sky and watched not one, but two red fire trucks pull up. I didn't see Melissa, but I had seen her leave and I was sure she was no longer at the party—there was, in fact, no more party to be at. Another pop sounded—much louder this time—accompanied by shattering glass. I hid in some bushes of the neighbouring house and watched the firemen with their hoses run into the house.

I never saw any flames, just smoke, black smoke, and lots of it. When the ambulance pulled up, my heart sank. I was certain no one had been harmed, yet I was still afraid. After a few minutes—it could have been ten or twenty; I hadn't brought my timer with me, so I could only guess—the ambulance drove off, empty, and I was relieved.

Back on Fairview Lane, I could see the black smoke in the distance and could still smell it too. Reflections of the fire trucks' spinning red lights bounced off the houses on the bottom of the street. Our house was untouched. Mrs Pomeroy stood at the end of her driveway, hands on her hips, and looked off at the smoke. I didn't think she saw me, but I couldn't risk it. I made my way home, cutting through the neighbours' backyards. I climbed up the drainage pipe to the second floor hallway, slipped in, and went straight to my room before my entrance could be detected.

I lay in bed, staring at the corkboard and its photos: all the same, our house (2.41 cm) with the Rockies (1.79 cm) not coming down on us but reaching up into the clouds. It took a lot of concentration to bring my breathing and my heartrate down to a normal pace. I would need to practice that more. I made a mental note.

***

On the last day of school, before the winter break, I made an ornament for Melissa: a snowman with dyed-black hair like hers and a wide grin like the one she used to wear. I hung it from her locker with a note: Merry Christmas, your loving brother. I wanted so bad to see her expression when she found it that I didn't care if I was late to class. I waited and watched from a dsitance until she finally appeared down the hall, walking slowly toward her locker with Frankie Stevenson at her heels.

She kept her head down and her shoulders hunched forward. Her feet barely left the floor but rather dragged as if invisible hands were clutching her ankles and trying to pull her back. She stopped at her locker and studied the ornament with a furrowed brow. My heart raced as I knew she would be happy when she read the note. Frankie said something to her which I could not hear, and Melissa shook her head emphatically. Then she read the note and darted a concerned look around her as if I had left her some ominous threat or something. She took the ornament, placed it in her bag, folded the note and stuffed it in her front pocket then hurried down the hall with Frankie doing his best to keep up. It was all quite strange and unsettling.

Something was wrong. Melissa and I would need to have a talk.

In our house, Christmas Eve dinner with honey smoked ham, green beans, and cranberry pie was the tradition. Mom was a great cook and even greater still when the holidays came around. Yet something was off that Christmas, off in the weather, off with Melissa, and it deeply affected me, too. I found myself on Christmas Eve with absolutely no appetite. What a terrible shame. I hoped there'd be some ham left over for when I was hungry, until then, I went to the dried-up creek to try and make sense of it all.

I watched from my hideout in the woods, but it wasn't fun. I should have been there at the table with them. There should have been snow on the ground. And Melissa should've had sandy-blond hair and unpainted nails. Suddenly and without warning, my thoughts went to Mrs Pomeroy. Her husband shouldn't have died in his shower. And her son shouldn't have run away.

Things were not the way they should have been, and that made me very angry.

***

I didn't get a tripod for Christmas. It didn't matter. I had gotten quite skilled at standing straight and still, chin at a 78° angle from the ground to make up for the slant of the street. I took a picture of the Rockies from the end of Mrs Pomeroy's driveway every day after school. I'd print it out, make the measurements, and when I found a particularly interesting aberration, I'd tack the picture onto my wall. (The corkboard was full with copies of the photo from July 16th—still the best I had taken yet.) By January 27th, my meticulous research was starting to pay off.

I wasn't sure who I'd share my findings with— probably Jimmy— but I pulled off the photos from November 8th and 16th, December 4th and 17th, and January 2nd and 27th; I placed them in a folder and put it in my backpack. I thought about showing Mom, but she was already so worried about Melissa—with her staying in her room all the time, not talking much, and listening to gloomy music—I didn't want to add to her troubles.

I took a seat with Jimmy, Kurt, and Edgar in the cafeteria. It had been a long time since I last spoke to them, but I pretended it had only been yesterday and the conversation was less awkward.

'Hey, Jimmy. Check out these pictures.'

I pulled them out of my backpack and handed them to him. I didn't explain. I wanted to see if he could see it for himself. Jimmy wasn't that smart, but who knew, he could surprise me.

'These are pictures of your street and the Rockies.'

'Yes, but look closely.'

He turned the pictures sideways and upside down and turned his head as well. 'What am I looking for?'

I took them from him and spread them on the table. Kurt and Edgar took an interest too, and the three of them looked them over trying to see what was so obvious.

'The sky's a different colour,' said Edgar. 'That's the only difference I see.'

'Look at the mountains,' I said.

Jimmy studied the photos a minute then shrugged. 'So. What is it? What about the mountains?'

I didn't lose my patience. I took a deep breath and spread out the photos in chronological order. Then I took out my ruler.

'One point six eight.' Next photo. 'One point six eight.' Next photo. 'One point six eight. One point six nine. One point six nine. One point seven.' I paused for effect before placing the ruler on the last photo. 'One point seven two.'

I leaned back in my chair and folded my arms.

Jimmy looked perplexed. 'It's just the camera angle. I don't get it.'

35

Kurt laughed, even though his mouth was full. Edgar leaned over the table to have another look then went back to his sandwich without a word.

'These pictures were all taken from the exact same location at the exact same angle.'

Jimmy looked at me with a raised eyebrow. 'The exact? Are you sure?'

I gathered the photos, put them back in my backpack, and stormed off. I expected more from Jimmy, but that was my fault. Photos or no photos, tripod or no tripod, no one was going to believe me.

I walked out of the cafeteria and headed to Mr Pervin's classroom. He was the smartest teacher I had, and before I gave up trying to share my discovery, I owed it to myself to at least consult Mr Pervin. That's when I saw Melissa, her head resting on the back of her hand flat against the locker.

'Melissa?'

She didn't turn.

I approached. 'Melissa, are you okay?'

She turned. Her eyes were wet. 'Oh, hi,' she said. She forced a smile. 'I'm fine. It's nothing.'

It wasn't nothing, but I didn't insist. I stood there looking stupid, trying to think of what to say. Melissa walked away before I could form my next question. It was going to be about Frankie, but I doubt she would have answered it anyway.

Seeing Melissa sad made me sad too. I didn't feel like showing my pictures to Mr Pervin anymore. I didn't feel like doing much of anything except maybe finding Frankie and having it out with him. That didn't happen, and after a few days I stopped looking for him.

It was more than the music, the make up, the painted nails, Cynthia Stansing, and Frankie Stevenson—Melissa was starting to get a label. After five straight days of wearing long sleeves pulled up past her wrists and onto the palms of her hands—a style Melissa had never worn before—people (stupid, mean people like Kevin Kramer) started to spread rumours about why Melissa was dressing that way. They were ugly rumours and they weren't true, so I set out to find Kevin and teach him a lesson about truth and family.

I confronted him at his locker. He told me to relax, that it was none of my business anyway. I shoved him, and hard, and dared him to repeat what he'd said. My fist was clenched and held high, and I was ready to pound the smug look off his face.

A small crowd had gathered around us. They encouraged me and cheered me on.

Mr Pervin intervened, stood between me and Kevin, and ordered the crowd to disperse. I was upset that a teacher had broken up the fight before it had really started, but I was most upset that that teacher was Mr Pervin who was my favourite.

He let Kevin go on to class, said he'd deal with him later, and he walked me to the principal's office. He kept silent the whole way and only turned and addressed me once we'd arrived.

I told him all the horrible lies Kevin had been spreading. I told him about the Rockies and about my photos, too. When I started to speak, it all came rushing out and I couldn't stop it: half sentences, isolated words with no context, even tears.

He said that he understood, though I couldn't imagine how. He said that I'd been through so much, more than any kid should have to go through. He said that he wasn't going to tell the principal but that I had to promise not to fight. 'Kids will do and say all kinds of hateful things,' he added. 'I don't know why they do it, but they do. You have to learn to let it go. Don't let it get to you.'

I wiped my eyes dry and nodded. Since I'd already blurted it out, I went back to the photos and asked him what they meant. He put his arm around my shoulder and walked me to my history class. He couldn't explain the photos; he didn't even try to. He simply told me to give it time, that in time everything would be okay.

At that moment, Mr Pervin was not my favourite teacher, but he didn't tell the principal on me so I kept my head down and my mouth shut.

When I got home, I tore up all my photos. At first it was a fit of anger, but then I regained control and continued to tear them up, slowly and methodically. I tore the photos in half, separating the Rockies from our house; then I tore off our roof then the rooms one by one. Usually it was fun to rip stuff up. But ripping up my photos wasn't fun. It made my stomach feel weird. I skipped dinner again.

I took a backpack full of ripped-up photos out to my hiding place in the woods. I had to walk all the way down Fairview Lane, down Ourc Street and across Willow Street to enter the woods then walk back up—all this to avoid leaving tracks in the snow. By the time I'd made it to the hideout, my family was finishing up their dinner. I arrived in time to see Dad toss a crumpled napkin onto his plate—that meant dinner was officially over—and Mom cleared the table. Usually Melissa helped, but that evening she didn't get up from the table. She sat there turning her half-filled glass in her hand, staring at the sloshing liquid. Dad got up from the table, gave Melissa a kiss on top of her head, and went to the kitchen to help Mom.

I left my hideout. I wanted Melissa to see me. I could make a silly face, and she'd smile and be happy again. But she wouldn't take her eyes off her glass. I was far from the window, but I made a tiny snow ball and threw it. Smack. Perfect aim.

Melissa jumped in her chair and looked around. I waved both my arms high in the air. She was looking right at me, but she didn't see me. *Turn off the dining room light, Melissa. I'm right here.*

Dad came back in the room, and he didn't look happy. Not happy at all.

Melissa said something to him and pointed at the window. Dad went to the light switch, but I scurried back to my hiding place and watched him put his face up to the glass, shield his eyes with his hand, and look around, his mouth twisted in an angry scowl.

Mom came back into the dining room. The three of them all pointed to the window, wearing angry, worried faces. *Go back to the kitchen. This is just between Melissa and me.*

Instead of heeding my telepathic request, Dad put on his coat, retrieved a large wrench from the garage, and came out to the backyard. He looked for footprints in the snow—of course there weren't any. He surveyed the brush that lined the woods but didn't come any closer.

When he went back inside, I breathed a sigh of relief. If he'd seen me, I would have been in big trouble. He closed the curtains to the large dining room window—I had never seen the curtains drawn before. The house looked as if in mourning, shut off from the outside world. I couldn't see them, and I panicked. I got up and ran through the woods back to Willow Street then walked calmly home.

The following night, the dining room curtains remained closed, and though I hadn't taken a photo of the Rockies to measure their encroachment, I knew that they were closer, much closer and taller still. The snow had started to melt, leaving patches scattered across the lawn. I timed myself, and from my hiding place, I could skip around the patches, run up to the kitchen wall, climb up the drainage pipe to the hallway window in under 14 seconds.

The hallway window was the only one without curtains or blinds, but there was nothing interesting to see in the hallway. I carried with me a long, thin stick, and from the ledge, I could reach around the wall and tap on Melissa's window. With her goth music on, I had to tap for a while to get her attention. Eventually, the music stopped, and I heard the blinds being pulled up. From the ledge, I couldn't see inside her window. I bet she was looking out, but she never opened the window to stick her head out so that I could see.

When the music came back on, I tapped again.

Close call. Instead of looking out her window, she stormed out of her room, down the hall to our parents' room. If she'd been looking to her right instead of straight ahead, surely she would have seen me. The game would have been over, and she would have been mad, and me, in trouble. But she didn't look right. And I breathed a sigh of relief.

As the weeks went on and the snow all melted away, the goth music coming from Melissa's room grew louder and darker, and the Rockies closer and taller.

I had to take action, and I did.

I burned for Melissa a CD of some of the nicer songs she used to listen to and sing along with when we lived in Boulder. I didn't think she'd listen to it if I gave it to her myself. So one night—at three o'clock in the morning to be exact—I climbed up the drainage pipe all the way to the roof, walked over to her room, and with my knee firmly dug into the gutter for support, I leaned over and slapped the CD—covered in sticky tape—onto her window.

Two nights later, the CD was still there. Melissa spent all of her time alone in her room, blinds drawn, and not even once did she look out the window. I threw pebbles at the window—many pebbles, some quite big—but she wouldn't look. Instead, Dad, with the biggest wrench he owned, came to the backyard.

He must have been cold in his pyjamas, but he stayed outside a good while. He even came into the woods, walked right by me, shouting threats and obscenities. I knew it wasn't nice, but it was also kind of funny. I had to pinch my nose not to laugh.

Unfortunately, it was Dad and not Melissa who spotted the CD stuck to her window. The police were called out, and they took the CD away. I hadn't taken any precautions, such as wiping away my fingerprints or anything, but I wasn't concerned. I was simply upset that

Melissa never got the chance to listen to the CD. I think it would have made her happy again. It would have reminded her of happier times when she'd sing and smile and when we lived in Boulder without Frankie and without Cynthia and without the Rockies towering over us.

I was sad but not discouraged. I'd make another CD, and I'd find another way to get it to her.

***

The following weekend, when I came home after playing down by the creek, Dad had an electric drill and was doing some kind of repairs to the outside of the house. I asked him what he was doing.

He shook his head and finished mounting a plastic keypad a few inches from the front door before responding, 'Unfortunately, my friend, I'm putting up a security system.'

I didn't understand what was unfortunate about that. Electronics are cool, and security is important.

'Why is that unfortunate?'

He lowered his drill and turned to me. 'Used to be these kinds of things were completely unnecessary.' He shook his head again. 'Times do change. Times do change.'

Just then, Mom came out. 'I'm heading to the store,' she said to Dad. 'Need anything?'

'Nope. Not that I can think of.'

I needed a new toothbrush, but I didn't say anything. I watched Mom drive away, then I turned back to Dad. 'Would you like some help?'

He finished fastening the keypad. 'All done. Thanks, though.'

Out of the corner of my eye, I caught Mrs Pomeroy peeking out of the curtains from across the street. She had that sad, concerned look on her face that always creeped me out. I put my gloves back on, covered my head with my hoody, and went back to the creek to play.

A few nights later, I discovered that Dad had also installed motion detectors around the house. They set off a siren that hurt my ears and caused many of our neighbours to come out of their houses. Even Mr Peterson, who I hadn't seen in months, stepped out in his pyjamas and slippers, wielding a baseball bat. I sat on the curb opposite our house, hands covering my ears. A policeman came, and Mom told him of all that had been going on the last few weeks: her daughter, Melissa, locked in her room, frightened by a late-night rapping against her window; rocks thrown against the dining room window while they were eating; footprints in the snow around the house. I listened and recognized some of the events as being my doing but not all of them.

The officer listened, nodded, and took down notes. When Mom had finished and Dad had led her back into the house, the officer walked over to me and addressed me. 'Hello there, son.'

'Officer.'

'Have you seen anything? Anything you can tell me about this late-night prowler?'

I rubbed my chin as if I had a beard, like someone in deep thought. 'I've been keeping a lookout, like all the neighbours. I guess I haven't been doing a good enough job.'

'Now, now, son. You mustn't blame yourself. Do you have any idea who could be doing this?'

Frankie Stevenson, Pete Hollbrock, Jimmy Spears. I shook my head.

'All right, then.' He put his notepad in his front shirt pocket. 'You get on back inside and get some sleep. It's late.'

'Yes, sir.'

I looked over my shoulder at the Rockies as I went back inside. The jagged peaks carved a twisted grin in the night sky. I wanted to punch it, to smack its stupid grin off its stupid rock face. But you can't punch a mountain. (I suppose you literally could punch a mountain, but that wouldn't do any good, would it?)

Spring was slow to come, but it came. The sun shone, the birds sang, but it got darker and sadder on Fairview Lane. Melissa now wore her hair so that the bangs hid her eyes. All colour except black and grey had gone from her clothes, her skin pale, her mouth frozen in a frown. Spring was a lie, a lie that fooled Mom and Dad but not me and Melissa.

The day after April Fool's, while talking to Billy Friedman who had the locker two lockers down from mine, Neil O'Brien said Melissa was hot and ready now that she'd gone goth. He started to say something else, but I didn't let him. I punched him in the face. I grabbed him by the neck and rammed his smug, sister-insulting little face into his locker. He tried to squirm free, so I kicked him in the balls and punched his mouth again and again and again and again.

Principal Lyons was not interested in why I'd done it. I was expelled.

At home, there was yelling and screaming like I'd never heard before, words running together that didn't make any sense. I was threatened with what Dad would do if he were around, then more yelling and screaming and tears, lots of tears.

It didn't matter what Neil had said or that I had to stand up for my sister. My camera was taken from me, I was grounded, and forced to see a psychiatrist. Worst of all, I was sent to a different school and there was no one to watch over Melissa. There was no one to protect her from Frankie and Cynthia, no one to fight off the rumours and the labels.

During the first session, I told Doctor Something-or-Other what had happened at school and why I had done what I'd done. For the second session, I stared at the wall, didn't say a word, not a one. The third session, I was also silent. There wasn't a fourth session.

May came and Dad installed cameras to go along with the motion detectors. He didn't do a very good job. One simply needed to walk through the woods, then hug the kitchen-side fence up to the garage and pass behind the first motion detector, then pull up by the window sill and slide along to the drainage pipe where there was access to the roof and all the upstairs windows of the house. I shouldn't have, but on two occasions, I made a smiley face on the hallway window with soap. It was a stupid thing to do. I thought I was being funny, but Mom wasn't laughing.

'It was me, Dad. I made the faces on the window with a bar of soap. And I'm sorry.' I practiced my apology in the bathroom mirror. The mirror didn't forgive me, and I knew Dad wouldn't either, so I kept my apology to myself. I did, however, promise to stop ninja-ing for a while. That didn't stop Dad from installing flood lights and tripwire in the backyard. He didn't do a very good job. I could have helped him, but he never asked.

***

Without a camera to record their movements, the Rockies took more and more liberties with their encroachment. Jimmy Spears said I was crazy. I got angry and pointed to the huge tower of rocks leaning over our street. 'Look at it, you idiot! Look at it! Open your eyes and see!'

He told me to leave him alone, and he ran away.

I saw Melissa sitting on the curb in Finley Square. I sat down next to her but not too close. I decided I needed to tell her. She was the only one who could see. She was the only one who would understand. I told her how the Rockies were coming, how they would crash down on us, and how I had watched and managed to keep them away, but now I was afraid things were slipping beyond my control.

She didn't say anything at first. She just stared at her hands and, with her thumb nail, scraped the peeling black polish off her other nails. After a moment, she looked up at me. 'You know. You're weird,' she said. 'But you're all right.'

I chuckled, and she scraped.

'Melissa, can I ask you something?'

She didn't answer at first, but when she was done scraping, she tugged on her long sleeves hiding her hands and said, 'I guess. What do you want to know?'

'Melissa, why did you dye your hair black?'

'That's what you want to know?'

I nodded.

She pulled at her hair. 'What? You don't like it?'

I shrugged. 'You had nice sandy-blond hair. That's all.'

She took to scraping her palms even though there wasn't any polish on them. 'You wouldn't understand,' she said.

I think she said that because she didn't understand, either, so I left it at that.

***

Four days before Melissa's birthday, the sun shone bright and full. It was a lie, and all the neighbours believed it. Mr Hamway threw a barbecue in his backyard. Technically, I was still grounded, but I was too good a ninja to be stopped from going out.

Jimmy Spears was at the barbecue. I didn't speak to him. Sandy Moreira and Pete Hollbrock were there too, but Melissa didn't show.

Mr Hamway asked me how I wanted my burger cooked. I told him I wasn't hungry, and I went to the creek to be alone.

I hid myself from the lying sun. I covered my ears, protected them from the lying laughter of my neighbours. I tried to remember Melissa's sandy-blond hair, and I cried.

By the time my eyes had dried, the noise from the barbecue had died down and dusk had settled over Fairview Lane. I didn't go straight home. Instead, I walked down to Finley Square. The grocery store was closed, and only three cars speckled the parking lot. They were not parked in the right places, and the mouth of Finley Square wasn't much of a mouth but a mostly empty space.

I turned onto Ourc Street and something smacked me on the cheek—smacked me hard—and it hurt. I rubbed my cheek and was hit on the head. It was like I was being pelted with pebbles from the sky. A few steps later I had to cover my head with my arms. Tiny white pellets were shooting at me from above. At first I thought it was just hail—and maybe it was—but hail in Colorado usually came in the afternoon or evening, not at night, and not without thunder. Whatever it was beat against the ground and the rooftops like war drums. I ducked my head and ran for home.

Once I'd reached Fairview Lane, the drumming was so loud I took my arms off my head and covered my ears. Sheets of white obscured my view. It was only from my keen sense of direction that I found my way home.

Melissa was outside under the front porch.

'What are you doing outside?' I shouted over the angry patter. 'Get inside!'

She didn't move. 'You were right,' she said. 'They're coming down on us, just like you said they would.'

I went to the middle of the street where I could get the best view of the Rockies. The thick torrents of white wouldn't let me see but a few inches in front of me. I spun in a circle, bombarded from all sides, seeing similar houses but not able to differentiate one from the other.

'Come on!' A hand grabbed me by the hoody and pulled. 'Come with me.'

I reached out and caught Melissa's hand and followed her home.

I froze at the front door.

'Don't worry,' she said. 'Come in. I don't bite.'

I crossed the threshold, looked left and right for Mom or Dad, but they didn't seem to be home.

'My God!' Melissa exclaimed, half laughing but wholly frightened. 'That's crazy.' She shook out her head, and little white pebbles flew from her black hair. 'Have you ever seen anything like that?' She brushed the bangs from her eyes, and her expression sobered. 'Oh my, you're bleeding.'

'I am?' I touched the sore spot on the side of my eye, looked at my finger, and saw blood.

'Come on.' She took my hand and led me up the stairs. 'We need to get that cleaned up.'

The sound of rapping against the windows covered the sound of our steps up the stairs. It filled my head and made me dizzy.

Melissa led me down the hall to her room, opened the door, and entered. I stayed in the hallway. 'Come on.' She waived me in. 'Or are you scared to be in a girl's room? I haven't bitten you yet, have I?'

I stepped in. Melissa's room was small and rectangular, like a coffin. The bed was flush against the wall, draped with a dark-blue quilt which clashed with the light-brown carpet. The walls were littered with photos and drawings and other disorderly scraps. I had never been inside Melissa's room, and it wasn't at all like how I'd imagined. I tried to remember what her room in Boulder was like, but no image came to mind and I was confused.

A small shelf next to the window displayed a row of vials of various colours: dark blues, yellow, black. Melissa opened a sliding closet door and rummaged for something while I walked over to the shelf for a closer inspection of the vials.

'What are these vials for?' I turned to see Melissa set a first aid kit on the desk.

'Don't worry about those,' she said, opened the kit, and pulled out a white cloth and another small unlabelled vial half filled with clear liquid.

'Why do you have a first aid kit in your room?' I asked.

She wet the cloth with the liquid from the vial and dabbed the corner of my eye. 'You ask a lot of questions.' Her sleeve was rolled up, and I saw that the ugly rumour Kevin Kramer had spread was true. I pretended not to notice and stared at my feet. She wiped from my eye to my temple and said, 'There. All better.'

'Thanks.'

'You want a Pepsi?'

I nodded.

The sky continued to smack against the window, and a particularly loud smack caused Melissa to jump. She threw a glance over her shoulder at the window then turned and tried—unsuccessfully—to blink away the concern from her face. She brushed by me on her way out the room then turned and motioned for me to follow. 'Come on. Let's go downstairs.'

I snatched the black vial from the shelf then followed her out the room.

'I saw that,' she said, but she continued down the stairs.

If I'd been a better ninja, Melissa wouldn't have seen me swipe the vial. I needed more training. I made a mental note.

In the kitchen, Melissa poured two tall glasses of Pepsi, took one for herself, and left me to take the other. I didn't take it. Instead, I rolled the vial in my hand and examined it. 'What is it?' I asked.

She snatched it from me. 'You've got grabby hands.'

'Sorry. It's just that it's beautiful.'

She looked it over then set it on the counter. 'It's not beautiful. It's dangerous.' Her eyes didn't leave the vial, and I wondered if she was talking to me or to it.

The rapping against the window grew louder, more violent still. Melissa looked over her shoulder then back at me. 'You wanna watch TV?'

She didn't wait for me to answer but walked out of the kitchen and into the living room. I followed.

Melissa plopped herself on the couch, grabbed the remote, and flicked on the TV: music videos, that melancholic, droning music Melissa never used to listen to.

The TV was in the wrong place. The couch was the wrong colour, the room had the wrong dimensions, and Melissa had an ugly, white bandage around her wrist that shouldn't have been there. I put my hands in the front pocket of my hoody. I didn't feel right.

'Melissa?'

'What is it?'

'Why is your wrist bandaged?'

'That's none of your business.' She turned up the TV. The sky rocks beating against the roof and the windows got louder as well.

'Melissa?'

She clicked off the TV, dropped the remote with a loud sigh, and turned to me. 'What? What is it this time?'

'Can I have the black vial? And the blue one I saw upstairs? I'll trade you for them.'

She picked up the remote, pointed it at the TV, but then just tossed it to the side where it bounced off the easy chair and landed on the floor. She stared at it a moment then answered, 'No, you can't have them. What do you want with them anyway?'

I shrugged even though she wasn't looking at me. 'Where'd you get 'em?'

'You ask too many questions.'

'I'm sorry.'

I stood there beside the couch, hands in my pockets. Melissa sat there staring at the blank TV screen. The patter against the living room window subsided, yet the occasional loud smack had Melissa twitch and shake. 'My doctor,' she said. 'I got them from my doctor, and they're dangerous.'

I wondered why a doctor would give her something dangerous, but I didn't ask.

Melisa stood and walked back to the kitchen. 'You haven't touched your Pepsi,' she called out.

I walked over to the kitchen door and saw Melissa staring at the black vial she was holding in her hand, the other hand wrapped around her drink. A smack against the kitchen window made her jump. 'Auugh! When will it end?'

'Melissa?'

She didn't look up.

'Melissa, I think I should go.'

Her bangs fell over her face, and I couldn't see her eyes. I turned and walked out the door.

I went over to the other side of the street and sat on the curb in front of Mrs Pomeroy's house. I picked up a handful of white pebbles that had fallen from the sky then looked to my right. The Rockies stood, far, far away.

I sat for a long while. I waited. Not sure for what; perhaps for the sky to stop falling; or for Mrs Pomeroy to come outside and lead me into her house; or for an ambulance to come. In any event, all three of those things happened and more or less at the same time.

'You shouldn't be out now,' said Mrs Pomeroy. 'It's cold, and you're grounded, remember?' She put her arm around my shoulder and led me up the driveway. I stopped and turned and watched the paramedics bring Melissa out on a stretcher. Strands of her black hair fell from under the white sheet.

'I want to go back to Boulder,' I mumbled.

'I know you do, son. I know. But give it time. With time, everything will be okay.'

THE WAGES OF INNOCENCE

'You have a visitor.'

I looked up from the table just in time to see that knowing, condescending twinkle in the orderly's eye. I didn't care. *Let him mock me. Jealous. Poor guy.*

I replied, 'Thank you,' but he'd already left.

The next sounds I heard were the click and smack of William Torenbow's dress shoes against the concrete floor echoing through the corridor. He could have walked more quietly, but then again, announcing his approach step by step did help build the anticipation. He knew that. It was part of the foreplay, and I did get excited. I sat on the edge of my seat, straightened my shirt, and put my hands firmly on my knees to keep my legs from shaking.

William arrived wearing a dark-grey suit—one I had never seen him in before. The pleats were still visible. It must have been his first time wearing it. He also wore a sky-blue silk tie—one I had complimented him on before. *This must be a big day.*

William flashed a wide smile, so wide it caused his glasses to slip on his nose. With an index finger, he pushed them back in place, then he cleared his throat. 'I've got big news for you today, Mark. Big. News.'

He took a seat in front of me, and our eyes locked. I don't know if I smiled at him or not. I was definitely smiling with my eyes, but today was orange-pill day, and the orange pills kept me from feeling my mouth—or my hands for that matter. Sometimes on orange-pill days, I'd catch myself twisting and pulling my fingers without even realizing. I could only wonder what involuntary muscle movements my mouth was making. William didn't seem to notice anything out of the ordinary, and he kept his eyes fixed on mine while he shared with me the 'big news'.

I wasn't really listening. When someone is excited and talking fast, their lips contort into the funniest of shapes, ever morphing, each transformation more comical and more outlandish than the last. It was really distracting, but I couldn't take my eyes off his lips.

'So, what do you think?' he asked. 'Is that the best news you've heard in a long time, or what?'

I laughed, and William laughed as well.

He stood, his smile beaming, his glasses slipping. He gave me a thumbs up—which was out of character for him—and said he'd be back.

'I'll see you next week, Mr Torenbow,' I said, and his forehead narrowed, and his visage stiffened.

'Mark?' He returned to the table, slowly pulled out the chair, and sat back down. 'Mark, did you understand what I just told you?'

I confessed I had been so happy I'd forgotten to listen. It was a stupid thing to say. I'd meant it as a compliment, but it came out all wrong. William was patient—he was always patient—and he placed his hands flat on the table and leaned in. 'Mark, you're getting out! Do you understand?'

'I'm getting out,' I repeated. 'I'm leaving. Leaving the hospital.'

'That's right.' He smiled and nodded.

'Am I going to jail?'

'No.' He shook his head and laughed.

It wasn't funny. I felt, after all I'd been through, that it was a legitimate question. He dismissed it emphatically.

'No. No. You are *not* going to jail. You are innocent.' His hands clenched into fists, but not aggressive fists, fists that one makes when the excitement is difficult to contain. 'You're getting out. Free! On with your life.'

I leaned back in my chair. 'Wow. That *is* big news.'

William's glasses slipped on his nose. He pushed them back into place then straightened his suit. 'Mark. Tomorrow you're getting out. Things may be difficult at first, but I'm not going to abandon you and I'm not going to abandon your case.'

'My case?'

'That's right, Mark. Your case,' he whispered. It wasn't a real whisper but a William Torenbow whisper that meant that what he had to say was extra important and that I had to listen with extra attention. 'It's not over, far from it. We're going to have to sue. You know that, don't you? We can't let them get away with what they've done.'

I stared at him and forgot to answer.

'You understand, don't you, Mark?'

I didn't understand. I didn't know who the 'them' was he was referring to. I think I nodded, but I said, 'No, no I don't understand.'

'We can't let the police get away with this.' He spoke of civic duty and something about the constitution being a muscle that needed to be exercised. I tried to remind him that today was orange-pill day, but the words came out wrong.

William nodded. Despite my stupid words, he understood me. He always understood me—even when I didn't quite understand myself. He took a deep breath and exhaled slowly. 'Now, Mark, I have to be in court tomorrow. Do you understand?'

'You have to be in court tomorrow,' I repeated—at least I think I did. That's what I meant to say, what I tried to say, but on orange-pill day I was never sure what sounds were inside my head and what sounds where outside my head.

'I won't be here when you're released.' He paused and exhaled through his nose. When William Torenbow exhaled through his nose, that meant he was sad or frustrated. I understood. I was sad and frustrated when I had to go to court, too.

'Is there someone I can call? Someone who can be here for you when you get out?' His lips pursed, and his head tilted to the left while he waited for me to respond.

I looked down at my lap and saw that I was pulling my fingers. This was a very difficult question to answer. There was Kevin. There was Tommy and Tommy's brother, Fred or Frank or some one-syllable name that began with 'F'. And there was my sister and her husband, Dan.

I looked back up at William Torenbow and shook my head.

'What about your sister?'

I looked back down at my hands, now pulling fingers two at a time. *What to say? What to say? I can't lie to William Torenbow, but if there was someone else, surely he would be jealous. He's done so much for me, been so kind. I can't break his heart.*

'Mark?' He leaned over the table. His hand touched my arm.

The orderly took a step toward us. 'Sir. No touching.'

William leaned back in his chair and nodded at the orderly.

Poor, poor William. Not allowed the simplest gesture of kindness and compassion. I smiled at him, I think.

'Mark? Shall I phone your sister?'

I shook my head.

'Is there anyone you want me to phone?'

I shook my head.

Surely he was relieved, though he did a good job not letting it show. Poor, poor William. Not allowed to express the most honest of emotions.

William sighed, pushed his glasses up, and rubbed his hands together. 'When you leave, they are going to give you some money. Not much, but …'

I looked at the orderly. He stood staring right at me with his hands crossed over his crotch. He always stood like that. Did he think I would look at his crotch? I couldn't have cared less about that ogre's crotch. What a weirdo.

'Mark?'

'Yes, William.'

'Do you know where you'll go? Where you'll stay?'

I had a pretty good idea, but I didn't say. That would have been presumptuous.

'I'm going to leave you the names, numbers, and addresses of a few decent hotels, not expensive, where you can pay by the week.'

My heart sank. Why would I stay at a hotel and not with him? But then I understood that he was just saying that because the orderly was there listening. I'd play along. I nodded.

'I'm also going to leave you my card.'

I smiled; hopefully it wasn't too wide of a smile.

'I want you to come to my office on Monday at ten in the morning. Can you do that?'

'Yes, William. I can do that.'

'But I want you to call me anytime before that if you're having problems, okay?'

'Okay.'

'I'll leave a phone with the check out. There won't be much credit on it, so only for emergencies, okay?'

'Okay.'

His serious expression gave way to beaming joy. 'You're getting out of here! Isn't that great?'

His joy was contagious, and even on orange-pill day, I knew I flashed a big, bright smile. He stood. I stood. I so wanted to hug him, but that would have to wait.

'Goodbye, Mark. Monday morning. Ten a.m.'

'Yep.'

The orderly escorted William out and touched him on the arm as he did so, just to rub it in. But I didn't care. Poor, sad, jealous man.

**

As I lay in my bed, I replayed the conversation over and over in my head. It had really happened. I knew it had. Later that day several orderlies had congratulated me on my upcoming release. I think they were actually happy for me. William had been so good at keeping his true emotions from showing, so I, too, remained calm and stoic. I said thank you to the orderlies but kept my enthusiasm in check.

It was very difficult to get to sleep. Not because tomorrow was blue-pill day, but because I was getting out! I was getting out! I was getting out!

**

On blue-pill day, I usually spent the morning in the common space, either playing checkers with Dr Hillside—who wasn't a doctor but would get irate if I didn't address him as such—or drawing by myself, if Luke wasn't hoarding all the supplies. But word had spread that today would be my last day, and everyone wanted to talk to me, some to congratulate me, some to ask for a favour, and some to warn me of lizard people or brain-washing radio waves or food additives that would turn me into a communist.

The attention was exhausting, but I maintained a smile and gave my ear to all who requested it. When pill-time came around, Mr Wiggles—the elder of the patients—escorted me to the front of the queue.

'No line on your last day,' he said. 'Those are the rules. No line on your last day.'

Scratchy Freddie only grumbled and contested for a second before giving up his spot at the front of the queue.

Nurse Crumb shook his head and waived me away. 'You don't get medicine. You're getting out.'

'No line on the last day!' Mr Wiggles shouted. He stuck his finger against the glass and poked and shouted and poked. 'No line on the last day!'

'No line on the last day,' said the nurse calmly, 'and no medicine on the last day, either.'

Scratchy Freddy pushed us both out of the way, and I had to hold Mr Wiggles back. He was very strong for an old man. I held him and hugged him. 'It's okay. I'll be fine. It's okay.'

I didn't get any blue pills—blue pills were my favourite—but at least I didn't have to queue at the canteen. Fish and rice: because blue-pill day was a Friday, and on Friday we had fish and rice.

After lunch, Doctor Schneider took me to checkout. I'd never been to checkout before, obviously, and I felt nervous. I always felt nervous before I got my blue pills, and I always got my blue pills before fish and rice. Today I'd already had fish and rice, but I hadn't had my blue pills, so I was extra nervous. Plus I was going to checkout, which was new. But Doctor Schneider was a nice man and he had a pleasant voice, and that helped a little—but only a little.

A small man with no hair on the top of his head, but lots of hair on the sides, gave me a black rucksack filled with clothes. The clothes were mine—boxers, socks, jeans, a T-shirt, and two dress shirts—but the rucksack wasn't. The short man said I could keep it anyway.

'It's a souvenir,' he said. 'Sign here.'

There was more: 160 dollars, a cell phone from William Torenbow, and William's business card with handwritten numbers and addresses on the back. I put the money and the cell in my trouser pocket and the business card in my shirt pocket next to my heart.

Doctor Schneider walked me to the front door, then through the gardens. 'Your lawyer, Mr Torenbow, told me there wouldn't be anyone to pick you up. Is that correct?'

'Yes, that's correct, Doctor.'

'Where will you go?'

I pulled out the business card and pointed to the first name on the back of the card.

'May I?' asked Doctor Schneider.

I let him look at the card, but I didn't let go of it.

'One seventy-two Wicks Road,' he said. 'That's on the other side of town.'

'It's a hotel,' I said.

Doctor Schneider nodded. 'I know it. You can take the bus. Number forty seven.'

I nodded like that meant something to me, but it didn't.

When we got to the gate, I stuck out my hand for the doctor to shake. He smiled and laughed out of his nose, shook his head, and put his arm on my back. 'I'll walk you to the bus stop. It's not far.'

The bus stop was just down the street from Beaumont Psychiatric Institute. I was pretty sure the five people waiting for the bus could tell we were doctor and patient because they gave us space and avoided eye contact.

When the bus arrived, Doctor Schneider bought me a ticket and asked the driver to tell me when I'd arrived at my stop. He extended his hand for me to shake and wished me luck.

Despite the kind doctors and nurses, I expected to feel disgust or anger or relief at the sight of the hospital disappearing into the distance, but I felt nothing. It was little more than a building and already a fading memory.

***

Since I was seeing William on Monday, I only booked a room for three nights: seventy-five dollars. The first thing I did was borrow an iron from the front desk and prepare my clothes for Monday: jeans and a white button-down shirt. The ensemble lacked colour; William liked colour, so I set out to find a tie. I could picture it in my mind: light pink with yellow stripes. I didn't know if William liked pink; he'd never seen me in pink so I was never able to gauge a reaction, but I knew he preferred soft colours. *Maybe I'll find a pink shirt and a soft-yellow tie.*

The neighbourhood surrounding the hotel was ugly. There were shops, but ugly shops that sold ugly things. I was not ugly; at least William didn't think I was ugly, and I didn't go into any of the shops. I walked and I walked until the ugly neighbourhood turned into one slightly less so. I passed many bars, and even though I was hungry and thirsty and tired of walking, I didn't go into any of them. I kept walking and looking and walking and looking until night fell and the shops closed and the bars started to fill up.

One ugly bar with an ugly neon sign over its ugly door had a beautiful sign posted in the window: Kitchen Help Wanted.

I had helped in a kitchen before, and if I got a job, oh how happy and proud William would be!

I entered and was greeted with familiar sounds and familiar smells. It was like I'd been here before, but I knew I hadn't. Still, it felt right, and I was comfortable. The tables and chairs on either side of the bar were wood, as were the floor and the walls. It was like I had stepped back in time, back to my time where I was meant to be: before the crime I did not commit, before the coerced confession, before the trial I pled out of, and before the institution.

On the left side of the bar sat two couples and a third wheel. The tables on the left were sparsely occupied, men and women—mostly young. On the right side of the bar, at the end, sat one lone man hidden in the shadows. The tables on the right were all empty; still, there was an odd symmetry to the place, as if that lone man had enough weight to balance the room all by himself.

I stepped up to the bar and waited for the barman to notice me. I stood straight like a statue, my hands flat against my sides. I bet the barman thought I was from the military, given my rigid posture and my institution-appropriate buzz cut.

'What'll I get you, sir?'

I fell at ease and pointed to the window behind me. 'I saw the sign.'

'Kitchen help?'

'That's right. I'm looking for work. Kitchen work.'

'You got experience?'

'Yes, sir.'

He looked me up and down, his lips contorted into something between scepticism and concession. 'Just a moment.' He left the bar and disappeared behind swinging doors, presumably to the kitchen: the kitchen where I'd soon be working!

He returned a moment later. 'Have a seat. The manager will be with you shortly.'

'Thank you,' I said, and I complied with his demand.

'Can I get you something to drink while you wait?'

'No, thank you.'

A few feet to my left, alone at a table, sat a young woman with pierced eyebrows and bright blue hair. The blue was slightly lighter than the blue of the blue pills, though that could have just been due to the contrast of the dark wood in the dimly lit bar. I tried not to stare, but it was hard not to look at the blue. It was always hard for me not to look at the blue.

She saw me stare, and she smiled at me.

I jerked my head back to the bar. Images of the blue still flashed before me. I blinked them away and concentrated, instead, on my posture. I'd always had horrible posture, and horrible posture says a lot about a man; it says a lot of unflattering things about a man: low self-esteem, poor work ethic—things that were well behind me, things that belonged to the old me, the pre-William Torenbow me.

I wondered if William's court appearance had gone well. I wanted to phone him and ask him, but the manager came and I had to concentrate on other things.

The manager's name was also William. He was far less handsome and far more corpulent than my William, but he was pleasant enough. He suspected I'd come from 'the joint', as he put it, and he said that wasn't a problem for him.

'I got a few employees come from the joint. Did their time and need a second chance. I believe in giving a second chance. Second chance, mind you, not a third. Understood?'

I nodded and told him that I understood, but that I didn't just come from 'the joint', but 'the hospital'.

'Hmmm.' He rubbed his chin and furrowed his brow.

'I have references, sir.'

'References?'

'From the doctors.'

He motioned with his hand. 'Can I see them?'

'Of course. I don't have them on me. I just happened to be walking by when I saw the sign. But I'm happy to go get them. I can be back in an hour.'

He waved away my words and shook his head. 'No matter. We'll worry about that later. I think it's best we try you out. Chris, the head cook, is the only reference I need.' He paused and waited for me to respond, but I didn't. 'When can you start?'

I beamed a smile. 'Right away, sir. I can start right away.'

He chuckled. 'Relax. Tell you what. Monday's a slow day. Why don't you come by Monday, say five o'clock? Chris'll show you the ropes, and we'll take it from there.'

I nodded. 'Sounds good.' We shook hands. William had a firm grip, but mine was firmer.

'You'll have a drink while you're here? To celebrate.'

'Oh, I'm not much of a drinker, but thank you.'

He waved away my words. 'Sean'll make you something with little alcohol. Sound good?'

'Sounds good. Thank you.'

William The Manager left me with a smile and said something to Sean The Barman on his way out the swinging doors in the back.

Sean pointed finger guns at me and said, 'How about tropical juices with a touch of rum?'

I thought it over, probably for longer than Sean expected, because he stepped up to me and repeated the offer.

I searched the ceiling for a response then found his eyes. 'Can you make me something blue?'

'Something blue?'

'Yes. Something blue. If you can. Thanks.'

With a tilt of the head, he replied, 'Something blue, coming up.'

Sean went off to make me something blue, and I couldn't help but hazard a glance over to the girl with the piercings and the blue hair. She was sipping something orange, then finished it in a gulp, stood, and walked over to the bar. 'Sean,' she called out, glass raised. 'I'll have another.'

I couldn't take my eyes off her, not because she was pretty—though she did have pretty hair—but because she wore loud clothing with lots of shiny things dangling from her ears, her wrists, and her belt. She flashed me a wide, disarming smile and plopped down on the stool next to me. 'Hiya, stranger.'

'And a hiya, stranger to you,' I said, giving her a two-finger salute.

'The name's Tchai.' She extended her hand which clinked and chimed with all the metal around her wrist.

I shook it but not with a firm grip like before, but delicately, like I thought I should. 'Tchai, like tea tchai?'

'Tchai like tea tchai,' she confirmed. 'And you, stranger? Or should I just call you stranger?'

'You can call me Mark. My name is Mark. Please, call me Mark.'

She put her palms up in a vertical 'halt'. 'Okay, Mark. I'll call you Mark.' She drummed on the bar and bobbed her head to music that was very different to the music playing in the bar. 'I couldn't help but overhear. You just got yourself a job.'

'Yeah, I did, didn't I?'

'Congratulations.'

'Thank you.' I smiled at Tchai. She was right, congratulations were in order. On my first day out of the institute, I'd found a job and a friend!

'I'd say that's something to drink to,' said Tchai.

On cue, Sean came back and placed two colourful drinks before us. He looked me in the eye and pointed to my drink. 'Sprite with a touch of Curaçao.'

'It's beautiful. Thank you, Sean.'

'And yours,' he said to Tchai, 'sex on the beach, extra sex, extra beach.'

'Thank you, Sean.' She raised her glass in a toast. 'Here's to your new job, Mark.'

I clinked her glass with mine and took a sip of the blue.

Tchai leaned in and whispered in my ear. 'You know, Mark, at first I thought you were a drug dealer.'

I had to set my drink down. Tchai had really taken me by surprise. My friend, Tchai, was always catching me by surprise. 'Do you mean, I look like a drug dealer?'

She looked me up and down with pursed lips and furrowed brow. 'Hmm, not really.' She leaned in again for another one of her famous only-for-me comments. 'Guess I'm just an optimistic kind of gal, you see?'

I took a bigger sip of the blue. What Tchai said made me sad, and I didn't really know why. Usually on blue-pill day I didn't get sad, but I had to get that out of my mind; it wasn't blue-pill day; there were no more blue-pill days. Today was Friday, not even fish-and-rice Friday, just Friday.

'You all right there, Mark?'

'Yeah, yeah. I'm fine.' I nodded and flashed her a smile.

'Looked like I'd lost you there for a minute.'

Tchai took a sip of the orange, and I stared into the blue. 'I'm just sorry I disappointed you, Tchai.'

She laughed. It was a loud, happy laugh, and I felt better. 'Now, now, Mark, chum.' She patted me on the back. It felt good. 'Don't you worry your pretty little head over that. There'll be drug dealers here, later. Always are.'

'Good. I'm glad,' I said, and I was.

'How's your drink?' she asked.

'Would you like to try?'

She took it from me. 'Sure, but you've got to try mine.'

Blue and orange! On the same day! I had to stop thinking like that, and I forced myself, despite everything inside me that was trying to resist, to take a sip of the orange. 'Hmm, not bad.'

'Yours doesn't have much alcohol,' she said. 'I prefer mine.'

I sat there at my new place of work with my new friend, Tchai, and sipped from the blue while she told me about all the charms on her charm bracelet: where she got them or who gave them to her, and what magical power each one had. I didn't think her charms had magical powers, and I didn't think Tchai thought her charms had magical powers, but they were fun stories anyway.

Tchai ordered another drink while I continued to nurse my first one. Sean offered to make me another, but I declined. I didn't want to take advantage of his kindness; I hadn't even started my work there after all, and I thought it would be wise to be on my best behaviour. Some time during our conversation, the bar had filled up—well, at least the left side of the bar had filled up. The lone man at the end of the bar to the right was still there, and still no one had dared to sit anywhere near him. I leaned into Tchai and whispered in her ear, just like Tchai was always doing. 'Hey, Tchai. Maybe that guy at the end of the bar is a drug dealer.'

'Nope. Definitely not.'

'How can you be so sure?'

'I can be so sure because a drug dealer is someone approachable, someone you can go right up to and say, 'Hey there, fella, I'd like some drugs'. And he says, 'Here you go. Here's some drugs. Enjoy.' And that guy over there is certainly not approachable.'

I nodded. 'I suppose that makes sense.'

Tchai took a big sip of the orange, and her eyes got real wide, and she shivered like she'd just been hit with a cold breeze.

'Hey, Tchai?'

'Hey, Mark.'

'Can I ask you something?'

'Ask away.'

'What kind of name is Tchai? I mean besides beautiful and original.'

'Aw, aren't you a sweetie pie.' She took my arm in hers and leaned in for a side hug the way good friends often do. 'It's short for Tchailenya, which means like 'blossoming flower' or something.'

'Tchailenya,' I repeated.

'Tchailenya Novetsylnova,' she said in a beautiful accent I hadn't noticed before.

I tried to repeat it and failed.

She tried to teach me how to say it, but I failed again. She had me take a sip of the orange, then I tried to pronounce her name once more. Better, but nowhere near as good as her.

'And you, Mark?'

'And me, Mark what?'

'Exactly.'

'Exactly how?'

'No, not how, but what? Mark what?'

I took another sip of the blue. Tchai wasn't making any sense.

'I can't call you Mark Stranger. You're not a stranger anymore.'

'Oh, right. I get it.'

Tchai punched me in the arm. It wasn't a mean punch, more like a wake-up-Mark punch. 'So?'

'Inendoff,' I said. 'Mark Inendoff.'

'Mark Inendoff. Mark Inendoff. Mark Inendoff.' Her eyes grew wider, her shoulders arched higher, and her back straightened as she repeated my name over and over again, like my name had magical powers and she was a monster coming to life by the incantation. 'Mark Inendoff!' She punched me in the arm again—hard, this time. 'You're that guy!'

'I'm that guy,' I repeated. 'What guy am I, Tchai?' I had to repeat the question to myself because it didn't sound like I was speaking English anymore and I was getting confused.

'You're that guy the police framed for that murder!' She immediately covered her mouth and looked around. Nobody was paying us any mind, and the music was loud. She leaned in anyway and whispered like Tchai always did. 'I'm right, aren't I?'

I smiled. Tchai was so happy with herself, I wished I'd had a big box with a big red ribbon in it to give her. 'Yep, I'm that guy. How'd you know?'

Tchai waved her arms wildly in the air. Charms clinked and bracelets rattled and Tchai looked at me with her mouth wide open. (Her tongue was orange from all the orange she'd been sipping.) 'How did I know?! How did I—' She put an arm around my shoulder. 'It was in all the papers.' Her other arm motioned to all the invisible papers spread out before us. 'The chief of police had to resign! It was a *big* story.'

Tchai looked around nervously again then covered her mouth. 'Sorry.' She leaned into my ear. 'I won't tell. Secret's safe with me.'

I leaned into her ear and whispered loudly, 'It's not a secret.'

This made Tchai giggle. Her bracelets and necklaces rattled and clinked when she giggled. She had a big smile on her face, and I was very happy.

'You're famous,' she said, and her smile widened.

Being famous is a wonderful thing. You can make people happy just by being there, just by sitting next to them, sipping from the blue. We didn't say anything for some time. Tchai drummed on the bar and stared up at the ceiling, lost in thought. I sat there next to her, being famous and making her happy.

'It's terrible what happened to you, what they did to you,' she said in a sombre tone that wasn't how Tchai usually sounded.

I took another sip from the blue.

'Those police officers were kicked off the force along with the chief,' she said, 'if that's any consolation. I suppose it isn't. Any consolation, I mean.'

'It's okay. I have a new life now.'

'And a new job!' Her face brightened the way her face often did.

'And a new friend.' I beamed, and we clinked our glasses again.

A song came on that I didn't recognize but that made Tchai jump out of her stool in excitement. She grabbed my hand. 'Come on. I wanna dance.'

'But our drinks?'

She waved away my concern, and we left the blue and the orange on the bar and headed to the space between the tables that served as a dance floor.

I'm a terrible dancer, always have been. But a famous person doesn't need to be a good dancer. A famous person can just stand on the dance floor and people will dance around him, happy just to be dancing in close proximity.

Tchai's smile was contagious, and I guess I must have looked pretty silly wearing that wide grin of mine because Tchai started giggling again, and all the metal on her clinked and chimed. Suddenly she stopped and pulled me near. 'See that guy over there?' She pointed to the dimly lit corridor in the back.

'I see,' I said, though I wasn't sure that I had.

'I bet that guy's a drug dealer.'

'You think?'

She nodded. 'I think.' She poked me in the chest with her index finger. 'Don't go anywhere. I'll be right back.'

She left, and I called after her, 'I'll be at the bar.'

I took another sip of the blue, and the blue was all gone. I waited for Tchai. I didn't touch the orange, even though it was just sitting there and I could have and Tchai wouldn't have minded.

She returned, and she looked disappointed.

'Well?'

She shook her head. 'Nope. Not a drug dealer.'

It was rare for Tchai to be sad like that, and it made me sad, too. I gave her a hug and a pat on the back. 'There, there. It's okay. We'll find a drug dealer soon. We'll find lots of drug dealers soon.'

Tchai took the orange and finished it in one big gulp. She slammed the glass back on the bar and turned to me. 'Let's get out of here. Go somewhere else.'

I started to say okay, but she was already pulling me along. 'Wait. I want to say goodbye to Sean.'

She turned and called out with a voice I wouldn't have thought possible from such a dainty girl. 'Goodbye, Sean. See you later.'

Sean looked up and waved to us. I waved back, and Tchai pulled me out of the bar.

'Damn! It's frickin' cold out.' She wrapped herself in her arms.

I wasn't cold, but I didn't have a jacket to give her. *Damnit, Mark!*

I wished I could have warmed her. I rubbed her back, but I wasn't convinced that was doing much good.

We hurried down the street, across another and down another still. We ended up at another bar. It wasn't a nice bar like the one I worked at, but Tchai said she knew the bartender.

'Heya, Gerald.' She stuck up a hand and waved. Even though the music was loud and the conversations around us louder, her charms clinked and chimed above the noise.

'Well hello there, beautiful.' Gerald was the bartender. He was a tall dark muscular man in a tight sleeveless white shirt. He, too, was beautiful, and he had a beautiful smile.

'Gerald, meet Mark. Mark, meet Gerald.'

We shook hands. It wasn't a firm handshake, like the kind that's appropriate when one is just hired at a new job, but a light, friendly handshake, like when someone meets a new friend.

Gerald turned to Tchai. 'What'll you have?'

'I'll have a sloppy orgy in the sand, and Mark will have …' She ran her fingers in her blue hair and fluffed it out some. 'Something blue. Sprite with Curaçao and rhum.'

Before Gerald could answer, Tchai pulled me through the crowd to the far side of the bar. When we arrived, our drinks were there, waiting for us.

'Wow, that was fast!' I said.

'Yep. Gerald's the best bartender in the world.' Tchai said it real loud so everyone could hear. We sat, clinked our glasses, and I took a sip of the blue.

Gerald's Sprite with Curaçao and rhum was a darker blue than it should have been, but I didn't complain. It tasted fine, and Tchai was happy, visibly much happier in this bar than in the last.

When Gerald passed in front of us to retrieve a bottle from the top shelf, Tchai asked him, 'Sam around?'

Gerald turned and, with his head, motioned to a group of men standing against the wall. Tchai furrowed her brow and squinted. Then Tchai's eyes got real big and wide, the way her eyes always did when she'd come to a realization. She leapt from her stool and bee-lined through the crowd.

Tchai was the only woman in the bar—at least the only one I could see in the poor lighting—and all the men stepped out of her way. I picked up the blue and the orange, cradled them against my chest, and followed.

Tchai threw her hands in the air and pounced on the back of some guy I hoped was named Sam.

'Samuel Sam Samonson!' she exclaimed.

He bent over so that she slid off his back and turned with a big smile. 'Tchailenya Tcha-Tcha Tchavsky!'

They hugged, and everyone around looked on with happy faces.

'Sam, I want you to meet my friend, Mark.'

'Hello, Mark.'

I said 'hi' back, but my voice wasn't loud enough to cut through all the noise. I knew I gave him a wide, friendly smile because I'd had very little orange that day and I could feel my mouth and I knew what it was doing.

'What are you guys up to?' Sam asked Tchai.

'We're celebrating!' Tchai threw her hands in the air again.

'Celebrating?'

Tchai put her arm around my shoulder. She was a head shorter than me, so she kind of pulled me down with her side hug. I clutched the blue and the orange, making sure not a drop was spilled. 'Mark got a new job!'

'Congratulations.' Sam raised his glass, and all the men around us raised their glasses. Everyone was happy for me. Everyone was proud of me, and they didn't even know I was famous.

Some guy asked me a question, but it was too noisy for me to make it out. I nodded and smiled, then he leaned into my ear and said, 'Pete'. He extended his hand for me to shake. I showed him the blue and the orange I was holding, and I smiled.

Pete continued to talk in my ear. I tried to listen, but Tchai's blue hair was right in front of me and I got distracted. Finally, Sam stopped talking to Tchai, and Tchai turned to face me. She could see that I was struggling. (Tchai was always very perceptive like that.) She said something to Pete, who smiled and nodded, then she motioned for me to follow her.

The dimly lit bar had a more dimly lit corridor in the back which led to a narrow staircase going up. Tchai bounded up the stairs two at a time. I was still holding the orange and the blue and didn't have a free hand to hold on to the railing. But I concentrated on each step and made it to the top with all the orange and the blue still in their respective glasses. To my surprise, the staircase opened to a well-lit room adorned with ferns and vines and hanging plants of various shades of green. There was no music or noise, and my ears could relax. Sofas and bean bags lined the walls. We took a seat on a plush sofa in the corner.

'Better?' Tchai asked.

'Better,' I answered. I handed her the orange. She said 'thanks' but looked less enthused than usual.

We didn't speak for a moment, and the few other people around us—three couples to be exact—merely whispered.

After a few more sips of the blue, I turned to Tchai. 'Tchai? Is Sam a drug dealer?'

She laughed. 'No. Sam is not a drug dealer. Sam's a friend.'

'Hmm. And Pete?'

Tchai shook her head. 'Nope. Pete's a friend, too. And Sam and Pete are married.'

Just because they were married didn't mean that they couldn't also be drug dealers, but I kept that thought to myself. I watched her sip the orange while I thought of what an eventful day I'd had.

Despite what she'd told me earlier, I didn't think Tchai's charms gave her the power to read minds. Still, she looked at me and said, 'It's been quite a day, hasn't it?'

I nodded. 'I found a job.'

'Yes, you did.'

'I made some friends.'

'Yes, you did.'

I watched her take another sip of the orange while I did the calculation in my head. 'I have four friends now,' I said.

'Friends are good.'

'Tchai, Sam, Pete, and William.'

'Who's William?'

'Ah, William.' I took a sip of the blue to mark my response with the dramatic pause it merited. 'William is my best and closest friend—has been for over three years now.'

'He stood by your side while you were wrongly imprisoned,' she added, though most likely from deduction rather than from any help from her charms.

'Yes, he did, Tchai. Yes, he did.'

Tchai took another sip of the orange, and the orange was almost all gone.

'I'm going to see him on Monday. He's going to be so happy that I found a job.'

'And that you've made some friends,' Tchai added with a wide smile.

I should have smiled back. Tchai's smile usually made me smile too, but I was suddenly wrought with concern. *Would William be happy that I've made friends? Is William the jealous type?* Oh, how I hoped he wouldn't be jealous. *Surely he could understand that though I had three other friends, he was still my best and closest friend, and no one would ever be able to come between us—not that my friends would ever try.*

'Are you worried about something, Mark?' asked Tchai. 'You look lost in thought.'

'I am worried,' I said. 'Though I doubt I need be. It's just that I don't really know if William is the jealous type or not.'

'Well, if he is jealous, then what kind of friend is he really?'

'You're right, Tchai.'

'I often am.'

'Still. He's had to wait so long for us to be together.' I stared at the ceiling and pondered my predicament.

'Were you and William together before ... before what happened to you?'

I shook my head. 'Actually, it was *because* of what happened to me that we met.'

'Is that so?'

I nodded. 'He was my lawyer.'

'Your lawyer?'

'Court appointed. And he always believed in me.' I started to tear up. Maybe it was in part due to fatigue, perhaps it had a bit to do with all the blue I'd been sipping, but once I started crying, I couldn't stop. I wiped my eyes, but that only made room for more tears to come flowing.

Tchai wrapped an arm around me and kissed me on top of the head.

'He believed in me when everyone else believed the police. Everyone else bought their lies and their 'evidence', but William continued to fight. To fight for *me*.' Tears were dripping from my cheek. I wiped them away with the back of my hand.

'William sounds like a good man,' said Tchai.

'William's a *great* man.'

'Is he why the FBI got involved?'

'You mean Internal Affairs,' I corrected. 'And yes, it's all because of

73

him. I don't know how he did it, but he did. Got them to retest the DNA. Got me out of that … that place. Got me freed.' I leaned back in the sofa and was overcome with exhaustion. Crying was tiring.

'When'd you get out?'

'What's today, Friday?'

'Yep, today's Friday.'

'I got out today.'

'No way!'

Tchai's exclamation startled me, and I jerked up, wide-eyed, alert.

'You got out today?'

'Yep.'

'Found a job and made friends! That's really impressive, Mark.'

I smiled. 'Yep, I did, didn't I? Found everything … everything except drugs.'

Tchai chuckled and slapped a hand on my thigh. 'Mark, don't worry about the drugs. If it wasn't meant to be, it wasn't meant to be.'

She tried to reassure me with a smile, but I could tell she was disappointed. I hated to see my friend disappointed. Even though I'd done many things already that day, even though I was famous, I hadn't been able to help my friend, and I, too, was disappointed. My eyelids grew heavy from the fatigue and the failure. I fell back in the sofa. My head smacked against the wall, but that didn't knock the sleep from me. I shook my head like a wet dog and slapped myself on the cheeks.

'Are you okay?'

I smiled at Tchai. 'Will you excuse me? I want to run to the men's room real quick.'

'Down the stairs. First door on the left.'

I handed her the blue to watch over and promised to be right back.

The stark contrast between the well-lit, quiet room with all the hanging plants and the dark, dingy corridor with the overflow of loud music and conversation was all quite a shock to my system. Usually the blue helped me resist such shocks, but again, I had to stop thinking like that. The blue I'd been sipping wasn't real blue—like Tchai's hair wasn't real blue and like Tchai's magical charms weren't really magical. But the disorientation I felt was real, so was the fatigue.

I pushed open the first door on the left, which wasn't labelled, and stepped in—a sink, one stall, and three men standing in the corner. The men's room was brightly lit, and the walls were covered in stickers and posters of all colours partially peeled or scraped off. I blinked and I blinked, but my tired eyes failed to adjust. I splashed cold water on my face. It felt good, like feathery fingers tickling my skin. I looked into the mirror; my eyes were bright red. I suppose it wasn't an unusual colour for someone who'd been crying like I had; still, it was a surprise. I almost didn't recognize the face looking back at me.

At the institute, it was always lights-out at 10 o'clock. I hadn't been up and about this late in over three years; I suppose part of me was asleep; part of me wasn't out and about, just like part of my mind was still back at the institute. I wasn't sure which part of my mind, exactly, wasn't with me, but I was painfully aware that I wasn't completely myself. I pulled down on the skin under my eyes. I wasn't sure what I was looking for in the base of my eyes; sometimes, I suppose, we just need to reassure ourselves that we're all there. There was a lot of red—not a surprise—but that didn't make me feel any more comfortable. We didn't have red-pill day at the institute; in fact, there wasn't much red of any kind in there. The patients and the staff never wore red. The gardens had no red flowers. Even the paints and the coloured pencils had no red, but I'd still come across it every now and then. Mostly in the eyes, especially when I'd pull down on the skin and look underneath the eyeball.

I splashed more water on my face, trickled a few drops in my eyes; that didn't help. Then I caught the reflection of two men in the mirror as they passed behind me. Their eyes, too, were red, but not a tired, been-crying red, but an angry, something-else red.

I slapped myself on the cheek—a bit harder than I'd meant to— straightened my shirt, and turned to head back to Tchai. A man in the corner, a short stocky man in a leather jacket, stared at me.

'Blow,' he said.

It wasn't until I was half-way up the stairs that it registered just what had transpired. He was offering me drugs! The very thing I wanted! The only thing I had yet to find that day.

I turned and went back.

'Need some blow?' he said when I re-entered.

'Yes. Yes, I do.'

He handed me a piece of folded-up glossy paper. 'Eighty bucks,' he said, and he winked.

I put the paper in my pant pocket, felt around for my money, but only pulled out a wadded-up cocktail napkin I had no memory of putting there. I heard the door open behind me, two men entered laughing, then immediately left. They, too, must have been disoriented.

'Hurry up, man.'

I checked my other pocket: empty. 'Shit.' I padded down my shirt, even though my shirt had no pockets. *What did I do with my money?* I started to go through all that I'd done that day. *Let's see. I left the institute with one hundred and sixty dollars. I gave the hotel, how much already?*

'Dude! Eighty bucks. Stop fucking around.'

'Yeah, yeah. Just a second.' *Then I went out to look for a tie. Did I buy a tie? Where is the tie I bought? Did I get something to eat? I must have. I'm not hungry. Or am I?*

'Fuck it.' He reached out his hand. 'Give me back the package.'

'Hold on. Just a sec.' *Tchai would have money. She wouldn't mind spotting me eighty bucks.* I turned and headed for the door.

A hand landed on my shoulder and yanked me back. It spun me around, and before I could get my bearings, a fist smacked my jaw. I stumbled back against the door.

The man grabbed me by my shirt—my good shirt! The shirt I was going to wear to see William—and he pinned me against the wall. 'You're not walking out of here with the package, you crazy fuck.'

He twisted my shirt with one hand while the other reached for my pocket.

I knocked the hand away from my trousers and pushed him, hard.

He fell back against the sink, tearing my shirt open in the process. Buttons flew from my shirt and rained down on the floor. One rolled underneath the stall, another landed at the man's feet; others still, I didn't know where they landed.

While I perused the floor, he punched me in the face. The room went black. Then he punched me again. He only had two fists—of that I am sure—still, I felt at least four, possibly six, fists wailing into me from all sides. I threw my arms over my head to shield it from the blows, and I was thrown into the stall. I landed on the toilet; something sharp and blunt jammed me in the back. My hand fell on something cold and metallic.

'Now, you're going to give me the package and the eighty bucks!' He stepped into the stall, fists clenched, eyes red and seething.

One hand covered my face; the other held the cold metallic toilet paper dispenser, loose, dangling from a rusty screw.

He yanked me up by the collar. I held fast to the dispenser, but it gave, ripped right out of the paper-thin partition.

He cocked back a fist. I swung the metal dispenser and knocked him on the head.

What a funny sound—funny like in a cartoon. The high-pitched ting reverberated in the small confines of the stall. I think it surprised him—the sound, not the hit which had little effect. He paused and looked perplexed. I hit him again, in the face. The edge of the dispenser tore through his skin, ripping a gash from his ear to his mouth.

He screamed.

I punched and slashed and slashed and punched.

He was hurt. I could have stopped; I should have stopped.

I didn't stop.

The metal dispenser clutched in my fist was my paint brush, his face my canvas. And there was no shortage of red. I slashed and stabbed until the angry streaks of red married into one bloody blot.

He fought back, or tried to, but I was quicker and stronger. His blood splashed me in the eye. I could not see, but I did not stop or slow down.

I heard—or saw, I cannot be certain—the bathroom door open. I dropped the dispenser, grabbed the man by the throat, pulled him into the stall, and slammed his head against the toilet.

What a strange sound that made—a loud thud, followed immediately by the crackle of his splitting skull—like the sound I imagined a fat man would make if he sat on a park bench, breaking it, then landed on a pack of potato chips.

I heard someone at the sink, whistling and washing up. Then I heard him leave.

The drug dealer lay sprawled out on the floor, head propped against the toilet, blood spilling out of his open skull into the toilet bowl. The stall partitions were streaked and sprayed with red. My shirt—my good shirt! The shirt I was going to wear to see William—was soaked in blood.

I don't remember what I did with the shirt; I must have taken it off, perhaps used it to clean up, perhaps I didn't clean up at all; I really don't remember. My next memory was me walking back up the stairs, checking my pockets to make sure I still had the drugs. I was relieved to find the folded-up piece of paper in my pocket and excited to tell Tchai the good news!

When I returned to the room of the hanging plants, I found Tchai sitting on the sofa talking to Sam, two glasses at their feet, one with the orange, the other with the blue.

Sam wasn't there when I left to use the restroom, was he?

I was very confused. So was Tchai from what I gathered from the look on her face. 'Where's your shirt?' she asked.

I looked at her then at Sam. 'Hi, Sam.'

'Hi, Mark.'

'Mark, what did you do with your shirt?' Tchai repeated.

I looked down. My bare torso glistened with water. Drops of red speckled my trousers. I got on bended knee and leaned into her ear. 'I got drugs.'

Her eyes widened, like her eyes often did when she heard good news. 'You got drugs?' she repeated.

I looked at Sam, who seamed to be pleased with the news as well, then back at Tchai, and I nodded. 'I got drugs.'

'That's great.' Her facial expression didn't mirror her words. Perhaps her magical charms were more magical than I'd given them credit for because she looked concerned. She tilted her head and furrowed her brow. 'Mark, is everything okay?'

I glanced over at Sam then leaned in again. 'Tchai, I think we should get out of here.'

Sam was the first one off the sofa, and he gave Tchai his hand to help her up. 'Gerald should have an extra shirt you can borrow,' he said to me.

'No,' said Tchai. She took my hand and pulled me toward the stairs. 'Let's get out of here. Now!'

We left the orange and the blue on the floor. I started to remind Tchai about our drinks, but she was hurrying down the steps, yanking me along with her, Sam following a step behind.

The noise in the corridor was loud, but in the main room it was deafening. I hadn't thought it possible, but the bar was more crowded than before. Still, everyone parted a path for Tchai and me to pass. I reached behind me with my free hand which Sam took, and the three of us bee-lined for the exit.

I didn't remember there being a bouncer when we'd arrived, but there was one at the door when we left. There were also about a dozen men outside queueing to get in. I got a few stares and a few smiles, though not because I was famous—because I was shirtless, and it was definitely not the right weather for me to be showing off my flat chest and pudgy abs.

'Aye, it's cold out here,' said Tchai. 'You poor thing.'

'I live around the corner,' said Sam, and before I could say anything, he was pulling me, Tchai attached, down the street.

It was fun—like a human train, and I was in the middle—but it didn't last; Sam really did live around the corner, four buildings from the bar, actually. The human train broke apart as we took the narrow steps two flights up to his flat.

Inside, Tchai let out a hooting sigh. I tried to imitate her, but my hoot was stupid.

'Whoooo-ah,' she repeated.

I tried again, and my 'whoo-ah' was much improved. Tchai was a good teacher.

'Mark. You're naked!' she said. She was smiling now, and the look of concern was all but gone from her face.

'Well,' I said. 'I've got my trousers.'

'What'd you do, trade your shirt for drugs?'

'Drugs!' I exclaimed. I reached in my back pocket for the folded-up piece of paper. Instead of drugs, I pulled out money: four folded twenty-dollar bills and a five-dollar bill. I laughed and laughed and crumpled onto Sam and Pete's living room sofa.

Tchai plopped herself down next to me. 'What's so funny, silly Mark?'

'I was looking for this.' I showed her the bills. 'Thought I'd lost it.' I reached into my front pocket and pulled out 'the package'. 'Ta-dah!'

Tchai threw her arms in the air. 'Yay! Drugs!'

Tchai was happy. It felt good to see her happy.

Sam returned with a black dress shirt. 'Here you go, Mark.'

'Thank you, Sam.' I didn't put it on right away. I felt dirty. 'Sam, may I use your washroom?'

He pointed to the hallway behind him. 'The bathroom's just down the hall. Feel free to use a towel or whatever you need. You can take a shower if you'd like, too.'

I was touched. Sam was such a nice man. 'That's very kind of you, Sam. Thank you.'

'Don't mention it.'

I did take a shower, a steaming-hot shower, the hottest shower I'd taken in nearly four years. I returned to the living room fresh-faced and bright-eyed. Tchai and Sam were sat on the floor around the coffee table, a sheet of black paper with four lines of coke in its centre was posed between them. I modelled the black dress shirt for them. They told me it suited me well. The sofa was vacant, so I plopped myself down and curled up in the foetal position, a cushion cradled under my weary head.

'We're going to wait for Pete, if that's okay with you,' said Tchai. 'He shouldn't be long.'

I smiled, and Sam smiled, and Tchai smiled, too.

'It's been a long day, has it?' asked Sam.

'Yes, it has, Sam. Yes, it has.'

'A long and eventful day,' said Tchai. 'He only got out toda—' She threw a hand over her mouth, her eyes wide like a deer's in the wrong place at the wrong time. 'Mark, I'm so sorry. It just slipped out.'

'Sorry 'bout what?' I said. 'I told you, it's not a secret. I'm among friends.'

'You've just got out,' started Sam, 'out of … jail?'

'Out of the hospital,' I corrected. 'Beaumont Institute, to be exact.'

'Oh.'

'Guess what Mark's last name is,' said Tchai. Her eyes were wide but with giddy excitement this time.

'What his last name is? I don't know, Beaumont?'

'No! Come on. Guess.'

'How should I know?'

'He just got *out*,' prodded Tchai. 'So, before he was *in*! Mark … In …'

'Mark In,' started Sam. Tchai encouraged him emphatically with her hands. 'In … In … Mark Inahospital?'

Tchai punched him in the arm. 'No, silly. Mark Inen …'

Sam just shook his head.

'Mark Inendoff!'

Sam shrugged his shoulders and twisted his lips in bewilderment. 'Is that supposed to mean something?' He turned to me. 'Sorry, Mark.'

I kind of shook my head, too tired to properly respond and tell him it was okay.

'Mark Inendoff,' Tchai repeated. 'Mark's the one the police framed for the murder of that guy in the bar fight! Remember?'

'Holy shit!' Sam exclaimed, like when someone's sitting right next to a famous person and are just realizing it. 'And they just let you out today!? That was like five years ago, right?'

'Four,' corrected Tchai.

'More like three,' I corrected. 'Three and a half, to be exact.'

'Holy Christ on a cracker,' said Sam. 'Wow.'

'Wow's right,' said Tchai. 'He got out today. And he's already found a job.'

'And friends,' I added.

'And friends,' Tchai repeated.

'How do the two of you know each other?' He was looking at Tchai when he asked.

'We met at Sullivan's Tavern. He went there to apply for a job.'

'And he got it,' said Sam

'And he got it,' Tchai repeated.

'Wow.' Sam turned to me. 'I'm so happy you're finally out, Mark. It's terrible what they did to you. I read about it in the papers.'

'Yeah, those bastards,' said Tchai. '*La Justicia Americana es una mierda.*'

'No doubt,' said Sam. 'Some cop bludgeoned his wife's lover to death in a bar, if I remember correctly.'

'Yeah,' said Tchai.

'And they framed you ... you! for it.'

I kind of nodded, too tired to really participate in the conversation. I'd heard the story many times already. William told me it and retold me it when I'd forgotten, and retold me it when I'd forgotten yet again.

Tchai's hand ran through my hair and down my cheek. I closed my eyes and thought of William.

'Do you have a place to stay?' asked Sam.

It took a moment for me to snap out of my reverie. I propped myself up on my elbow, waited for the blood to flow down from my head, then sat up. 'I'm staying at a hotel until Monday. Then I'm staying with William.'

'I hope it's a nice hotel,' said Sam. 'After all you've been through.'

'It's not,' I replied. 'It's over by ... over by ...'

'Mark?' Tchai sounded worried.

I looked at her and smiled. 'I don't remember where the hotel is.'

Sam pulled out his cell phone. 'Do you know the name?'

'It had like a French name, Le Luxe, or something like that.'

Sam typed away on his phone. Tchai rubbed my leg with a gentle hand.

'I remember it was right next to a pawn shop.'

'Do you remember the name of the pawn shop?' asked Sam.

'Pete and Sam's, or Sam and Pete's,' I said with no conviction.

Sam stopped typing and looked at me with a brow raised. 'Sam and Pete's?'

I shook my head. 'No, that's not it. I don't remember.'

'The Luccin?' asked Sam. 'On Waverly?'

'That's it! Wow, Sam. How'd you do that?'

He waved his cell. 'Magic.'

'Hey!' said Tchai. 'You cheated.' She jingled the charms on her wrist. 'I've got magic. You used your phone.'

'Same difference,' Sam responded.

I flopped back down on the sofa, my head resting on top of my locked hands, and I stared at the ceiling. 'Anyway, it'll do, until Monday.'

'Then Monday, you're staying with your friend?' asked Sam.

'William,' added Tchai. 'He's a good man.'

'He's a *great* man,' I corrected.

'I'm glad you have a good man in your life,' said Sam. 'I mean, a *great* man in your life.'

I smiled.

'How'd they do it?' asked Sam. 'I mean, why'd they pick you?' I started to answer, but Sam added, 'If you don't want to talk about it, that's cool. I get it.'

'No. That's okay.' I shifted onto my side so I could better look at him while I spoke. 'It was a tough time in my life, back then. I was out under the overpass, out by Bleaker. You know it?'

'By the glass plant?'

'Yeah.' I paused, and I remembered. 'I don't know. I was staying out there, then one night the police came. They said I'd killed a man. Took me to the station, interrogated me for hours and hours and hours.' I remembered, and I shuddered. 'They told me all kinds of stories. Said if I'd confess, they'd make it all go away.'

'Bastards!' Tchai exclaimed.

'I didn't know what, exactly, to confess to. But they helped me.'

'Damn,' said Sam. 'That's messed up.'

I could feel the tears coming back, but I fought them off. 'Then I met William.' I lay back down on the sofa. Tchai's hand ran through my hair. Sam came around the table, sat down beside me, and took my hand in his.

'I'm really sorry that happened to you, Mark,' he said.

I shook my head. 'It's not your fault. Plus,'—I beamed a smile—'if it hadn't, I would never have met William.'

'Damn,' said Sam, turning to Tchai. 'After all that, and he still manages to find the positive.'

'I find everything,' I mumbled.

Tchai laughed. 'That's right. In one day, you found a job and new friends.'

'And drugs,' I added. 'Don't forget the drugs.'

'Oh, I haven't. Speaking of which, where's Pete?'

'I'll give him a call,' said Sam.

That was the last thing I heard before I dozed off. I don't remember dozing off, but I must have, because the next thing I knew, Tchai was shaking me by the shoulders. 'Mark. Mark.' Her voice was a song, and her charms clinked in rhythm as she shook me lightly. 'Mark. Look who's here.'

My eyes shot open. I thought somehow, some way, William had found me. He couldn't wait, so he came looking for me and he found me.

'Hi, Mark,' said Pete.

I admit I was a bit disappointed. But at the same time, it was nice to see Pete again. I sat up and rubbed my eyes. 'Hello, Pete.'

'You were talking in your sleep,' said Tchai.

'Was I?'

She smiled and nodded.

'What did I say?'

'You said, 'Hi, William.' Then you mumbled for a bit. Then you said 'Hi, William' again.'

I chuckled. Tchai beamed, her face filled with excitement. 'Pete's here,' she said.

'I know. I just said hi to him.'

'Pete's here,' she repeated then leaned into my ear. 'That means we're going to do drugs!'

I took a strand of her hair in my hand. I let the blue slip through my fingers. 'I'm okay. You guys go ahead.'

'What? Are you sure?'

I nodded. 'The drugs are for you, Tchai. I'm tired. I'm going to go back to sleep and dream about William.'

'You can take the bed,' said Sam. He pointed down the hall. 'You'll be more comfortable there. Really. I put clean sheets on this morning.'

I lay back down on the sofa. 'I want to stay here with you guys, if that's okay. You can do what you want. Trust me. Right now, I could sleep through anything.' I didn't wait for a response. I couldn't wait for a response. Sleep came for me at once, and I did not resist.

I dreamt of William; I'm sure I did, though my sleep was too profound for me to remember any of the details. When I woke, I was lying in Pete and Sam's bed under a warm, puffy quilt. I stretched and yawned, got up, and stretched and yawned some more. I went to the bathroom to wash my face. I was wearing a black dress shirt that I didn't immediately recognize, and the reflection looking back at me in the mirror didn't really look much like me at all—at least not the me I expected.

I stepped out of the bathroom and stood in the hallway a moment. To my left was the living room, and though the shutters were closed, quite a bit of daylight bled in. A few photos hung on the hallway wall: photos of Pete and Sam and other people who looked like friends. It was a very strange sensation waking up somewhere other than in the institute. I stood there awhile longer, not knowing where to go, and not sure if I had the energy to go anywhere, anyway.

I heard the sound of cupboards being opened and closed and dishes clanking and silverware rattling. I only remember listening; I don't remember walking, but I must have, because then I was standing at the threshold, watching Tchai set the table in the kitchen.

She turned and saw me standing there. 'Well, hello, sleepy head.'

'Good morning, Tchai.'

She laughed through her nose. 'Try 'good afternoon'.'

'Good afternoon, Tchai.'

'Good afternoon, Mark.' She went to the sink and washed a frying pan. With her back to me and the water running, she said, 'I can't decide if I want to make omelettes or cook these turkey breasts I found in the fridge.'

'Where are Pete and Sam?'

She shut the faucet and faced me. 'Sam had to go to work. Pete went out to get some stuff. He should be back in a few hours.'

I took a seat at the kitchen table. My head was heavy, so I held it up with a hand and propped my elbow on the table.

'Juice?' said Tchai.

Before I could answer, Tchai set a tall glass of orange juice before me.

'Yellow!' I exclaimed. I looked at Tchai in amazement. 'How did you know?'

She tilted her head and gazed at me, perplexed.

'Yellow always comes after blue. How did you know?'

She pursed her lips and searched the corners of her eyes. Then she looked back at me, raised her arms, shook her charms, smiled, and said, 'Magic.'

I took a sip of the yellow. 'I don't believe in magic. I think it's just a coincidence.'

Tchai didn't respond. Instead, she went back to her pots and pans and turkey breasts and eggs. I stared into the yellow. The yellow was never my favourite. The yellow made everything bright and clear. It made me remember, and it made me sad.

'I think I'll make omelettes,' said Tchai. 'Fancy a cheese omelette, Mark?'

I didn't respond. Instead, I sloshed the yellow in its glass and watched it settle.

'Mark?'

I looked up. 'Yeah. Cheese omelette. Sounds good. Thanks, Tchai.'

The first time William told me that Internal Affairs was looking into my case was on a yellow-pill day. That was the day I started to understand, the day I started to remember: how the interrogating officer clenched my testicles in one hand and gripped my wrist with the other; how he dictated all the gruesome lies I was to put down on paper; how he had me believe I was a violent lunatic that needed to be put away for life; how he regretted the state had no capital punishment to mete out to me.

The problem with the yellow was that, although everything became clear, I was unable to care, unable to get angry. 'Mark, the confession was coerced,' William had told me. 'The DNA evidence was planted. You didn't do those things. You didn't hurt anybody. You aren't a violent man.'

I listened. I understood. I felt nothing.

'Here you go, Mark,' said Tchai, and she set a plate before me. 'I didn't exactly manage the flip. The omelette always breaks when I flip it. Always.'

The yellow omelette was split in two, and yellow cheese bled from its centre.

'Thank you, Tchai,' I said, and I took a sip of the yellow in my glass.

Tchai sat down across from me and began to eat. I went through my trouser pockets and laid the contents on the table: four twenty-dollar bills and one five, a wadded-up napkin, and William's business card.

'You never did tell me what you did with your shirt,' said Tchai.

I didn't respond.

'Doesn't matter,' she said. 'You can keep that one. Pete won't mind. I'm sure.'

I looked down at the black dress shirt I was wearing. It wasn't the dress shirt I had planned to wear to see William. It wasn't the right shirt. I knew what I'd done with the right shirt, and despite all the yellow I'd been sipping, I did feel; I did care.

'So, what are your plans for the day?' asked Tchai.

I picked up the yellow in my glass but set it right back down and looked up at my friend. 'Tchai, I need to use the phone.'

'Sure.' She got up, left the kitchen, and came back a moment later with her cell. 'Here. Use mine.'

'Thanks.' I phoned William.

He answered on the first ring, and my heart jumped. I didn't know if it was from excitement or fear. I suspected both.

'William. Hi. It's Mark.'

I got up from the table and went to the living room to be alone with William.

'How are you doing, Mark?' He sounded so distant, so formal, so official.

'William, I think I'm in trouble.'

In the three and a half years I'd known William, there was nothing he would deny me. I never really asked him for anything, but he had a way of reading me, of knowing what I needed, and he'd do anything and everything he could to help me. Now that I was free, it was supposed to be my turn to do everything I could to give *him* what *he* needed. I was disappointed and embarrassed. I felt I had fallen short. I knew I had fallen short.

'I'm sorry, William. I'm truly, truly sorry.'

I gave William the address, and he came for me. He always came for me.

I sat on the living room sofa, my head stuck in the vice of my hands, and it was Tchai who greeted William at the door.

'Hi, I'm Tchai.'

'William Torenbow. Pleasure to meet you.'

'I've heard so much about you. The pleasure is all mine.'

Tchai's magical charms weaved their magic, and Tchai read my mind—mine and William's as well. She left us alone in the living room and stayed in the kitchen, presumably doing the washing up.

'Mark? Is everything okay?'

I peeked through the cracks of my fingers. William wore a dark-grey suit with a sky-blue tie: the one I had complimented him on before, the one he wore when he had good news to give me. He took a seat on the sofa next to me. 'Mark, you said you are in trouble?'

'I found a job,' I blurted out. This didn't provoke the happiness I wanted but rather confusion.

'A job? That's … that's great.'

'I made friends.'

'Like Tchai?'

I pulled my head out of the grip of my hands, rubbing my cheeks as I did so. 'Tchai, Pete, and Sam. Pete and Sam are married. This is their flat.'

William looked at me; I looked at him. He adjusted his glasses, opened his mouth as if to speak, but didn't. I couldn't read him. I became quite nervous and took to rubbing my hands up and down my legs.

'So, everything's—' He started, but he didn't finish his thought.

I pulled on the edges of Pete's black dress shirt and tears poured from my eyes.

William touched me on the arm. 'Mark, what is it? What's the matter?'

My head fell onto his shoulder. 'I'm a terrible man,' I said between sobs.

'No, you're not.'

'I am. I killed a man. I bludgeoned him to death in the men's room of a bar.'

'Now, now.' William patted my shoulder. He took my hand in his. 'Mark, you need to listen to me, and listen to me closely.'

I wiped away my tears, but more tears took their place.

'You are a good man, Mark. An innocent man. You have to stop talking like this. You did nothing wrong.'

I slouched further into the sofa. My head now rested in the crook of William's arm. 'I'm not, William. I'm a terrible, violent man that should be locked up. Locked up forever. It's too bad the state doesn't have capital punishment to mete out to me.'

'No, no.' He squeezed my hand. Tears blurred my vision, leaving me only the blue of his tie in sight. 'You mustn't talk like that. It's not true, Mark. The police killed that man, not you. You are *not* a terrible man. I won't let you talk like that.'

With my free hand I reached for the blue. It was soft and silky smooth. 'I should be punished.'

'Shh. No one's going to punish you. I'm not going to let them lock you up. You hear me? Do you hear me, Mark? I'm not going to let them lock you up.'

The doorbell rang. I did not get up. I did not look up. I kept my eyes on the blue. 'They're here for me,' I mumbled. 'They're coming to take me away.'

'Shh, Mark. Shh. Everything's going to be okay. I'm here. Nobody's going to take you away.'

I TOUCHED A DEMON
ON THE CHEEK

2 November 2018

My hands have a mind of their own.

I knew I shouldn't smoke—well, my mind knew I shouldn't smoke, and it knew I didn't even want to.

My hands, however, reached for the rolling papers.

I yelled at them to stop. Do you think they listened?

They lined a leaf of paper with tobacco, and they packed. They sprinkled in some PCP, cocaine, and hash. They rolled and they sealed, ignoring my repeated instructions to the contrary.

'I swear, you light that thing up and I'll make you pay!'

Do you think they worried?

They didn't so much as hesitate. They grabbed the lighter, sparked a flame, and burned off the wick of the joint.

I turned my head, but my hands are fast. They rammed that thing in my mouth, and lest I suffocate, I was forced to take a drag. Before I had even blown out the offensive smoke, my hands were already shoving that thing in my mouth again. Oh, how I did suffer!

I waited for my hands to set the joint on the ashtray, then I instructed my arms to drop to my sides. I stood from the sofa and ran to the wall, turning at the last second so that my right hand would smack against it. Unfortunately, my shoulder took the brunt of the contact. My shoulder! What had my shoulder ever done to me?

If my hands had mouths, surely they would have laughed.

'This is not funny, and it's not over! Far from it.'

My obedient legs carried me toward the bathroom and stopped just shy of the doorway. I leaned against the wall such that my arm dangled at my side, my hand—my insubordinate hand—flush against the door jamb. 'I tried the easy way. Don't say I didn't warn you.'

My foot (oh, how I love my feet) kicked the door, slamming it shut on my right hand.

I screamed a scream of pain but also a scream of dominance. I would make my hands see. I would make my hands obey.

With my foot holding the door closed, I leaned back, crushing the hand further into subordination. 'And I'll do the same to you, left hand!'

My eyes shed tears—surely tears of joy at the victory of my rational mind over the irrational one of my hands.

My left hand was spared the same fate, for the time being, but I did smack it against the wall in case it thought my warning a bluff.

I returned to the living room and took a seat on the sofa. On the coffee table before me sat the half-smoked joint balancing on the side of the ashtray. I was surprised to see that the joint was still burning. Surely it couldn't still be, yet there it was.

I had to lean in to get a better look, as often the mind will play tricks. A thin stream of smoke rose to touch my nostrils. The nose doesn't always know and is often in collusion with my lying eyes, so I leaned in even more. In doing so, I felt the heat of the ember, and my lips brushed the butt of the joint.

My mouth has a mind of its own.

***

I heard a steady 'beep' coming from my left. I lay there and listened. I tried to open my eyes, yet they were heavy or glued shut somehow. I found I had neither the force nor the will to insist. The 'beep' faded out, and the orange of my eyelids faded to black.

A steady 'tap' 'tap' sounded from far away. As it grew nearer, my eyes slowly opened to a haze of white. The 'tap' was accompanied by voices, 468 voices to be exact. As the voices grew louder, the white gave way to soft blues and metallic greys. I blinked, and a shot of pain rang through my head.

'You're up. Perfect timing.'

The image of a man in a white coat flashed before me then was replaced by a swirl of blues and greys.

'Don't try to force your eyes. Give it time.'

The 'tap' 'tap' ceased, and a different voice spoke. 'Is he awake? Can we speak to him now?'

'Let's give him another hour.'

***

My eyes opened to waves of white. Two pillars of black fluttered to my left.

'Mr Werner?'

I lay and I watched the forms quiver, more and more slowly, then stablize. The waves of white became a sheet covering my body; the pillars of black, one man and one woman, both in business attire.

'Mr Werner, how are you feeling?' The voice came from my right.

My head refused to move, perhaps I had forgotten how to ask it to.

'Mr Werner?'

'Where am I?' It was my voice, though I felt no movement in my mouth.

'You're in Saint Luke's Hospital. The detectives would like to ask you some questions. Would that be okay?'

'I can't move.'

'That's normal. You're still feeling the effects of the sedatives. Don't try to fight it. But can you answer some questions? It will only take a minute.'

A hand came to me from my right and touched my forehead. From the corner of my eye, I saw a man in glasses dressed as a doctor. He leaned over me and peered into my eyes. He wore concern on his face, which quickly dissipated, then I saw him nod to the detectives and leave.

'Mr Werner, I'm Detective Brandly,' said the man, 'and this is my partner Detective Anders. Can you tell us what happened?'

I tested the extent of mobility in my eyes, yet the sharp pain in my temples forced my gaze to remain straight ahead.

'Mr Werner, we're with the Special Victims Unit,' said the woman. 'We know what happened. We just need a word from you, and we can put a stop to it.'

I tested the mobility of my fingers. I saw them twitch—well, I saw the bandages twitch—yet I felt nothing. 'I have nothing to say to you.'

'Mr Werner.' The woman took a step toward me. 'We see this every day. It won't stop until you make it stop. It won't just go away.'

I couldn't move my legs. They were hidden under the sheet, presumably. I felt nothing but pain in my temples and rhythmic explosions of pain in my jaw.

'He'll do it again,' said the man.

'Who?' I asked. 'Jonathon?'

'We can have him behind bars,' said the man. 'We can make it so that he never hurts you again. Please. Tell us what happened.'

'Jonathon didn't do anything.' Feeling slowly returned to my neck while the two detectives renewed their plea, each time with more urgency and more prophesies of escalating violence. I was able to turn my head slightly, enough to see the row of drip bags behind me where clear liquids oozed through plastic tubes on their way to my inert arms.

'Mr Werner,' said the woman. 'We can't help you if you don't let us.'

A feeble laugh escaped my mouth. 'That's what Jonathon always says.'

***

The hospital, like the police, is a noble yet flawed institution. The doctors and nurses, though honourable, are short-sighted, with a blind focus paid to the corporal, often to the detriment of the mental and the spiritual. In their unwarranted dedication to eradicating my body's suffering—my body! as if it merited such sympathy—they pumped me full of codeine, morphine, zetabaxalodine, extra-hyper-anti-defililsaturaloxonine, and other concoctions known only by symbols and equations. My blood was fortified, mineralized, oxigenitized, gluco-syrino-patholipsonified and treated with agents known only by metaphors and allusions.

For forty days and forty nights I lay in a sterilized room, covered in a sterilized white sheet, deprived of the suffering I so deserved.

One after the other, men and women in white suits came to the foot of my bed. They asked me how I felt, how I'd slept, and noted my answers on clipboards which they left for their colleagues.

A doctor who presented herself as *my* doctor informed me—with a smile!—that I was making a full recovery.

'Doctor,' I said. 'You have a decidedly strange notion of the word 'full'.'

In guise of a response, she Latinised to a nurse who stood by my drip bags then turned to me and said, 'You have a visitor. I'll send him in shortly.'

There were no clocks visible from my bed, and the light in the room, artificial. Yet from the regular 'drip' 'drip' 'drip' that marked the seconds, I understood that it was one hour and seventeen minutes later when Jonathon came to see me.

We said nothing to each other while he stood at my bedside perusing the machines and the bags and the tubes and the bandages with numbed incomprehension. Finally, he looked me in the eye, turned his hands palms up, lifted his shoulders, and said, 'What am I supposed to do?'

I'll admit the question had never occurred to me. I twisted the corner of my mouth in what would have to pass for a shrug.

'I can't keep going through this with you,' he continued. 'I want to help you but—' He sighed and stepped away from the bed. 'Actually, I don't even know if that's true anymore. I don't know if I *want* to help you.' He gazed upon me for a reaction, yet I'd been far too anesthetized—and this, before being admitted to the hospital—to engage him on the level he was at.

'Anyway, I'm going to Switzerland with Sean and Frederic.' He sighed. His eyes found a comfortable spot on the wall above my head. 'A couples getaway turned into a one-couple and a third-wheel getaway. Again. But I'm not going to cancel.' He took in a deep breath and exhaled slowly. 'I'm not going to clean up your mess anymore.' He shook his head. 'No, I'm done cleaning up your mess. When I return, I'll be staying with Sylvia. At least until I find my own place. You can have the apartment—if you manage to make the rent. Too many unpleasant memories for me there. I'm moving on.' His eyes found mine. 'I wish you would, too.'

'Say hi to Sean and Frederic for me.'

A spit of air escaped his lips, and he turned and walked out the door.

***

I returned to our apartment—scratch that, *my* apartment—on Saint Mark's place, wounded and weary from a long, bloody battle. I felt myself the victor, not having smoked a cigarette—let alone PCP—in weeks. Do you think I received a hero's welcome? I was many things. But heroic? I think not. And in as much as there was no friend or lover to welcome me, the lifeless, one bedroom apartment welcomed me with an indifference I must admit was reciprocal.

I felt Jonathon's absence immediately and in a way I was not prepared for. I did not miss him on an emotional or carnal level, like I had expected, but rather on a spacial, material one. His artwork and photos, which once adorned the walls, had been taken down, leaving rectangular patches of unstained paint to further expose the yellow nicotine residue that coated the walls. He had taken the bookshelf and the entertainment system—I had no need for them—but in their place hung a heavy void. The kitchen had been cleared of all its culinary gadgets and tools (oh, how Jonathon loved to cook). The cupboards and drawers were bare, save a lone set of dishes, one knife, one fork, and one spoon.

Jonathon, as was his nature, did leave the apartment clean. It reeked of sprays, ammonia, and bleach, yet the kitchen counter and the bar that separated it from the living room already showed a thin layer of dust.

Jonathon had spoken of 'unpleasant memories' that lingered in the apartment, but as I explored the space, I found little trace of our past there together.

I'd returned in the early afternoon of a bright August day. The mockingly named 'living' room was bathed in sunlight. I set my bag down in the centre—where the rug used to be, the one Jonathon had brought back from Tunisia—and promptly shut the stores and drew the curtains.

I sat on the sofa and contemplated the emptiness.

I did not get up until nightfall, when I could move about in the purest dark the apartment would grant me. I feared my idle hands, and rightfully so. Though the right one was still wrapped in a thick bandage, I doubted that would be enough to stifle its mischievous nature. I endeavoured to scrub away the nicotine stains that marred the walls: a task that would not only eradicate some of the ugliness I had left on the apartment but also tax my body, lest it get complacent and undeservedly pampered.

My right hand was unwilling to hold a sponge, so I scrubbed with my left and wrapped a rag around my bandaged right hand which was tasked with the wiping. Not two minutes into the work and my mind was solicited, nay, begged for respite. 'What the walls need is a fresh coat of paint. Best leave it till tomorrow, after a quick trip to the hardware store.'

I dismissed the suggestion immediately. *Always the easy way out! And why not a massage and a hot bath?*

'So much physical stress, so soon after getting out of the hospital!'

And, whose fault is it that we were in the hospital?

I scrubbed and wiped while I argued with my aching muscles and aching joints. Cigarettes, hash, and PCP had been but the beginning. I could feel other urges, other malicious schemes being concocted by my traitorous body; my arms had tingled and twitched in hospital at the preparation of a morphine injection; my eyes had lingered that extra beat on the bottle of pills; my tongue had slipped ever so slightly out of its confines when I passed a bar on the way home not five minutes after my release. I knew, even then, that my destructive cravings were planning another assault. And oh though my muscles protested, there would be no rest for the wicked. *Rest is for the righteous! If you do not submit through teaching, then it shall be through toil!*

It was only when the first light of day crept through the cracks of the stores and encroached into my dark quarters that my mind caved in to my body's demands and I crawled to the couch and collapsed into slumber.

***

I held no illusion that my job at the vintage clothing shop, Back Rack Vintage, would be waiting for me. I also had no illusion that the landlord would simply forget about me or pity me or absolve me of my responsibilities toward him. The little bit of self-pride I still possessed,

I abhorred: the last vestige of the delusional. I swallowed, and I walked, head held as high as my stiff neck would allow, to the shop.

Back Rack Vintage had been doing well before my hospitalization. Vintage clothing was in high demand. Consumers not wanting to be subject to the fashions of the day sought out those of the past. Now vintage was the fashion of the day. I could identify with those consumers: running from something only to recreate the very thing they were running from.

A vintage clothing shop was, thus, the perfect place to work for a drug addict: not because most of the staff moonlighted as dealers, but because the job consisted of supplying an illusory need. Though fashion was far less harmful than narcotics, it was equally as illusory; the satisfaction it provided, just as fleeting.

The music of Fela Kuti played softly from the speaker by the till. Eddie was deep in the second of the four racks, putting articles back in their place. I took only two steps in, enough to let any customer enter or leave, and stood by the doorway waiting for him to notice me.

Once he had finished straightening the rack, he did look up. I saw in his eyes first fear, then repulsion, followed only a long moment thereafter by recognition. 'Eddie, my friend,' I said as I approached. 'How goes it?'

His eyes could no longer stay on mine. He went back to the rack he'd just attended to and gave it another straightening. 'So, you're out finally. You look like shit.'

'Eddie, my friend,'—I entered the aisle slowly—'always a kind word.'

He turned to me and found the stomach to look me in the eyes. 'I hope you're feeling better than you look.'

I took another step. Now at arms length, I stopped. 'It's true, there's room for improvement.'

'So, what brings you by?'

'How's business?'

'Never better.' A customer entered, and Eddie begged me, with a gesture, to excuse him.

I did turn to let him pass, but he chose to go back and around the rack to take a separate aisle.

'Can I help you find anything?'

I watched in the round surveillance mirror hanging in the corner. Eddie was small, and his customer smaller.

'Just browsing,' she replied without looking up.

'If you need anything, just let me know.'

'Thank you.'

Eddie took up post behind the till; his eyes searched the sidewalk beyond the open door in the hope, surely, of finding another distraction.

I walked back the way I'd come and stopped at the counter. 'I'm looking for work.'

Eddie exhaled slowly. 'I hear Guildie's on Eleventh is looking for a barback.' He took his eyes off the door to sweep by mine on the way to the lone customer in the back. 'You know. Just till you get back on your feet.'

I couldn't tell if he was trying to rub salt in my freshly opened wounds. Work at a bar! The belly of the beast! Or did he afford me more willpower than he rightfully should have?

'I don't drink anymore,' I said. 'But I don't think it'd be a good idea for me to work in a bar. At least not for a while.'

He nodded. 'You've got a point.'

'How about a few shifts here? Who's opening now?'

Eddie exhaled slowly again, turned, and looked me up and down. 'No offense, but I can't have you working here. You're not exactly the face that's going to get people in to buy clothes, are you?'

I wasn't offended but angered and perplexed. He could have cited the shifts I'd been late for, or the times I didn't come in or phone, the missing money, clothes sold with no receipts. But he cited my face, the abhorrence of my very appearance as reason to refuse me another chance.

'Well then, Eddie, if that's the way you feel about it.'

'Why don't you get some rest? Come back when,'—he ran an open hand in circles inches from his face—'when you get better.'

'Goodbye, Eddie.'

I left my pride with the other relics in the shop and lumbered home.

***

Eddie was right about one thing: I would need to get better before I could find work. The landlord would simply have to wait.

I entered the apartment and was immediately stricken with a violent twist and tug in my stomach. Always hard to tell if the discomfort was from hunger, craving, or withdrawal, but I'd learned they were essentially the same thing: my body making demands and inflicting me with pain until I caved in. Like a petulant child that had been raised with no boundaries, no discipline—the remedy was the same: tough love, zero tolerance.

I'll feed you when I decide to feed you. A little fast will do you good.

In response, the sharp, pulsating pain in my jaw spread to my teeth. The stabs locked in rhythm to my heart, each beat a blow to my mouth followed by a slight delay then a prick in my fingers, as if the blood running through me were knives targeting my extremities.

I'll admit, I was weakened. I collapsed onto the couch and curled up on my side, one hand clutching my stomach, the other clutching my jaw. I tried slowing my heart. I tried holding my breath. I tried sheer willpower, anything to prevent my arteries from arming my enraged nerves.

A minute passed wherein I withstood the incessant assault. Another minute went by, and I had not given in. The pain spread to my groin, and my bladder begged for release.

I laughed.

You'll have to do better than that. What did you expect? That I'd get up and go to the bathroom to relieve myself?

I laughed some more.

The bathroom! Where, in the medicine chest, are bottles of pain killers. Ha! Do you take me for a fool?

With one hand still holding my jaw, the other slid from my stomach to my trousers. I undid the button and the zipper, then I had to pause as the effort, combined with the pain, was dizzying. I took my time and slowly pulled my trousers down to mid thigh. I wiggled over to the side of the sofa, aimed, and relieved myself on the living room floor.

A mop and some cleaning product—I'll deal with that tomorrow.

My bladder could trouble me no more, and I was still on the couch, the pills still in their bottles tucked in the bathroom's medicine chest far away. *Who's the clever one now?* I laughed and I laughed and I laughed. *Score one for Michael.*

Even with the pounding pain, sleep eventually came for me. It was a troubled sleep, troubled with dark, indecipherable images, troubled with vague dreams wherein something resembling Jonathon colluded with something resembling my own body. I awoke sticky with perspiration. My stomach, no longer content with churning and pulling, had balled into a fist and was trying to punch its way out. A sharp, bitter stench of urine wafted into my nostrils and began poking around my head, unplugging things and plugging them back in the wrong place. I rolled over and heaved, which awakened a legion of hammers that had amassed at my temples.

I'd been here before: heroin. For seven days and seven nights. Jonathon had been with me then. He had knelt by my bedside. He had held my hand and wiped my brow. I knew the man presently kneeling beside me next to a puddle of my own urine was not Jonathon but a mere projection of my tortured mind. It was a blessed solace to me all the same, one I did not shun or try to rationalize away.

I put a cupped hand on his cheek.

His eyelids drifted shut. The corners of his mouth floated upwards. His face conformed to the crook of my palm and cradled itself therein. I started to speak, but he breathed a 'shhh'; the breath tickled my wrist as it left his lips. I, too, shut my eyes. I, too, parted my lips into an open-mouth smile. My head found his hand for support which lowered me gently into sleep.

I awoke in bed. The curtains were partially open, and the bright afternoon sun filled the room. My last recollections were of the afternoon, in the living room. I did not know how I'd got into bed, but I surmised that I must have been there for about twenty-four hours. It felt like I'd been asleep for days, weeks even. All soreness in my body was gone; my head was clear; my eyes had no difficulty, no reluctance in opening.

I slipped out of bed and stretched my naked body. The sun was not my enemy, so I went to the centre of the room to greet it as a friend. I searched my memory for what had transpired after meeting Jonathon in my waking dream but was convinced to 'Let it go. Enjoy the moment.'; advice I followed for nearly a full minute.

My memory had tried to hide many things from me before, none of them good.

With quivering steps, I started for the door. The last desperate pleas of my guilty mind—'Find out later. Stay here in the sun. Be happy, for once.'—did not leave me unaffected, and my steps slowed progressively as I made my way across the room.

My hand gripped the doorknob, and I became just as stiff. It was not the cajoling of my subconscious which finally arrested my movements, but fear. My mind had all but conceded the cover-up, and the pieces were slowly returning to me: the street, the shop, the binge.

It required both of my arms and a heavy head to pull the door open enough for me to slither through. To my left, the kitchen; straight ahead, the living room—the first thing that occupied my sights was the mop bucket, with the mop handle sticking out, leaning against the sofa. The blinds were drawn, but slivers of light bled through the cracks and glistened off the clean, lemon-scented wood floor.

Jonathon would have never left the mop out. And he did say he was done cleaning up my mess. What have I done?

The answer was in plain sight. I needed only turn my head to the left: hamburger wrappers and candy wrappers, wadded up and spread out along the kitchen bar, along with an empty bottle of pills. A white plastic bag hung from a cupboard door handle. I could see plates and glasses piled in the sink. I took a trepidatious step in.

Below the sink, two tall beer bottles—40 ounces each—lay on the floor. I shuttled past them sideways, afraid of any inadvertent contact. I snatched the plastic bag from the cupboard door handle and tore it open. Empty, save for a receipt: the itemization of my relapse all in black and white.

I dropped to my knees and covered my face.

'There must be another explanation,' my mind pleaded, despite the mountain of evidence.

I grabbed one of the beer bottles by its neck, shot up, and hurled it against the wall. 'Liar!'

The bottle shattered. The tip, with its jagged neck, bounced off the counter and rolled to my feet. I bent and picked it up. My balled-up hand wrapped tight around its neck; the sharp points of transparent brown glass stuck out of my fist as if I were strangling a serpent, forcing its mouth open and its fangs to jut out.

My knuckles turned white. My fist shook from the concentrated effort. I yanked my arm up, bringing the jagged glass to my temple. 'You fucking traitor!' My rational mind was all that I had left, but alas, it, too, had been corrupted.

My head tilted away from the glass, while my hand clutching the weapon followed. 'Do you remember now, you filthy liar!'

My memory gave me a fleeting image of me walking down the street to the shop. Nothing more.

I stuck the glass against my temple and pressed, hard enough to draw blood. 'And the money! How did you pay?'

I didn't wait for an answer—it would have probably been a lie anyway. I threw the broken bottle neck across the living room where it hit the floor and skidded into the corner. I spun in a circle, searching for my clothes, then stormed back into the bedroom where I found my trousers neatly folded in the top dresser drawer. There was a five-dollar bill and some loose change that I tossed out the window. The credit card would receive a more thorough, more deserving treatment.

I ransacked the kitchen, the living room, and the bedroom, looking for a pair of scissors. I knew I'd seen a pair, on my first day back, in the drawer with the knives. But they had vanished. Anger clouded my better judgment—my better judgment! Always so easily clouded—and I did step into the bathroom to look for the scissors.

I found them in the medicine chest, along with six of the seven bottles of painkillers I'd returned from the hospital with. I cut the credit card down the middle, then I cut those two pieces, then those four, until I was cutting tiny blue plastic scraps, too small for the large thick-bladed scissors.

My shredded credit card went down the drain. Good riddance! Then I turned my attention to the more challenging front-door/lock-and-key situation. I couldn't very well lock the door then chuck my keys out the window, though I did give that option its due consideration. Eventually, once the battle was won, I'd need to be able to leave the apartment, and the fire escape demanded a certain agility I doubted myself the possessor of, much less given the condition I expected to be in several days from now.

Apparently, the threats against my rational mind had succeeded in making it my ally once again, as common sense did return to me and presented me with a more reasonable approach to my dilemma. I would lock the door and hide the key (somewhere accessible, though with difficulty, providing me with various obstacles I'd need to overcome, thus giving my mind many opportunities to re-assess the need for the key).

After trying out many spots, I settled on the toilet tank. It would require me to remove the heavy lid, submerge my hand in cold water, retrieve the plastic bag—triple-tied—and then extract the key from the putty I wrapped it in—putty I'd peeled off the base of the shower. It didn't stick, but I weaved it around and through the key multiple times so that only a cool head and calm hand could free it.

I deliberated long and hard over what to do with the remaining beer bottle. Ultimately, I washed it out and removed the label—though it still looked like a beer bottle with its beer-bottle shape and beer-bottle transparent brown glass. I filled it with water—the only substance I'd allow my treacherous body—and returned to the bedroom. I closed the blinds and drew the curtains. Satisfied nothing could interrupt me, I crawled into bed and prepared for battle.

I would not fall for the sweet, loving Jonathon vision again. If reason were to forsake me and delusion were to summon him once again, I would not look into his soft eyes but snap his skinny neck. I had to stay one step ahead and prepare my moves now while I still enjoyed some clarity of thought.

In the past, fear had been my downfall: fear of loneliness, fear of life without a crutch, fear of pain. Now, with clarity of thought, I welcomed those fears. I was alone, without a crutch; bring on the pain!

My body wasted no time in complying. First, the pain started in my teeth, then it spread to my jaw. I had neglected to dispose of the pain killers. Intentional? I trusted no one, not the pangs in my body and especially not my conniving mind. I lay in bed, deliberating whether to get up and flush the pills down the toilet, but I did not fall for such a pedestrian ploy. *Sure, I'll go to the bathroom and open the pill bottles. Is that what you want me to do?* I laughed. *I will not be had so easily. I will not step foot outside this room. Bring on the pain!*

The dull, invisible drills that were burrowing through my teeth and jaw penetrated the right side of my neck, causing it to stiffen and my shoulder and arm to tense up. A minute later, possibly several hours, there was manifest in my body a perfectly symmetrical duality: the right side, crippled with pain, stiff and unable to move; the left, free from sensation, relaxed and unhindered.

I did not know why this was. It was unexpected, and I failed to find what advantage my body thought it would gain from such a state. A minute later, or perhaps hours, I began to entertain the notion that perhaps I was winning this battle—the veteran that I was—and that the guiles of my diseased body had no effect upon my left side. I concentrated on where the pain was at its weakest, my right foot, and tried to will it away, mind over matter, as they say. And within minutes, or perhaps hours, I had succeeded. Pain is, after all, a message from one's body to one's mind. I knew not to listen to my body—oh, the tales it would tell. I simply replaced its message with a more truthful one of my own: this pain is not the suffering of my body; it is a lie spewing from the lips of a demon to whom my body has given over its voice.

I had to resort to simplistic metaphor to make my mind understand. *You must not listen to anything it tells you. This demon is no conduit to any deity. Its master is a vulgar, carnal thing, a thing of need and hunger and thirst. This demon seeks to feed. We shall then make it starve. This demon seeks to survive. We shall then ensure that it soon dies. Only then will our body be free and we can be one again.*

So sound was my reasoning, such was the strength of my conviction, that in minutes, or perhaps hours, the demon had reign but over the right side of my face and neck. My shoulders, arms, and legs moved about freely, unaffected by the demon's deceit. The war was not over— far from it—but I had won the battle. With the comfort and confidence of this assessment, I shut my eyes and waited for the recompense of a well-derserved sleep.

The room was much the same when I awoke, impossible to tell day from night. Yet the bed was no longer centred but flush against the wall. It did trouble me that I had no recollection of having moved it—a benign gesture, possibly, but it could have been something entirely different, as recent events had demonstrated. I needed to take further precautions against these unchecked, unremembered somnambulations. I tore the curtains from their fastenings then rolled them up, and like laces through sneakers, I snaked them in between and around my legs then tied them tight. Any attempt to get out of bed would have me faceplant to the floor.

I was a clever one. I foresaw each of my enemy's attacks and took ingenious measures to protect myself from them. I did not, however, think my enemy would be defeated so easily. It would take at least seven days and seven nights to starve the demon, and I was only in day two— or thereabouts.

The pain in my jaw, having been thwarted in its crawl down my body, proceeded upwards to concentrate behind my right eye. My beating heart provoked a stabbing sensation which could not be ignored yet, I found, could be alleviated by applying pressure to my eye with the base of my palm pushing against the socket. In addition to dulling the pain, this also produced flashes of black, red, and orange which popped before me then quickly dissolved. A man of less reason might see, in these flashes, the form of a lover, a friend, or a father figure. Even I, in the peak of mental clarity, saw a black silhouette which resembled my late not-so-great father and believed, but for a brief second, that I was being visited from beyond the grave. The form gave way to swirls of orange and red that condensed into the smiling face of Jonathon.

I was not fooled—though at first I pretended to be, only to have some fun. 'Jonathon, oh Jonathon. You've come back.' I reached out to the shape, wrapped my hand around its thin black neck, but it vanished before I could squeeze.

I removed my palm from my eye, and a torrent of fists and knives and sledgehammers came rushing from the back of my head to pound and slash and strike their way through the front. I had no recent injuries to account for this level of pain—my last hospital stay now well in the past. I had to conjecture that the demon inside me was at its wits' end and was making its final, frantic attempts to hold ground. This realization brought me much joy, a joy that increased as the pain increased until pleasure and pain merged into one writhing and prolonged climax.

I closed my eyes. When I opened them again, I was visited by Hunger. Like a claw ploughing through my entrails, lunging and grasping, it was a welcome distraction from the throbbing in my head. I lay there, contemplating my hunger, until it grew bored and left.

Next, the demon conjured for me Thirst.

Thirst was a breeze of sand that filled my lungs. Tiny dry particles attached themselves to the inside of my throat and itched for my nails to come tearing through the flesh in relief. The air I reluctantly breathed in stoked the embers of my irritation. I burned.

A label-less, transparent-brown beer bottle sat on the nightstand, and my memory tried to convince me that it had been filled with water.

'Do you take me for a fool!?'

My memory conjured up images of me filling up the bottle at the kitchen sink, along with the recollection of thought processes not dissimilar to my own. Quite convincing, I'll admit. But Thirst was keeping my other cravings away, so I decided to host it for as long as I could. Even the demon needed to drink, and as long as it was begging me for water, its other demands, more noxious demands, would receive no advocate.

The fast should have brought with it the added benefit of not having to relieve myself. This, oddly, was not the case, for my true body, my long buried and addiction-riddled body was beginning to crawl out of its toxic confines, purging—by any means, by any orifice—itself of the contamination. The lack of mobility in my waist and legs made even urinating off the side of the bed a chore. After a while, I saved my energy for more important tasks and took the fact that I was lying in my own piss and excrement as a testament to my resolve, proof of my inevitable victory.

The pores on my skin opened, dumping out the filthy by-product of this intense biological warfare. The smell was of boiling decay. I heaved, which ripped my arid throat with violence, yet I could feel it slowly soothed by what I assumed to be blood. My next heave confirmed the thought.

The demon left my teeth, left my jaw, and my eye, and focused its assault on my throat.

'Bring on the pain!'

I knew I would eventually have to drink, yet I did not trust my memory of filling up the bottle with water, nor did I trust my eyes and nose to inform me of what the bottle was currently filled with. I trusted myself to go into the kitchen or the bathroom even less. *In the bathroom, there are pills. And in the kitchen, who knows what trap the demon has set for me there?*

I wiggled my way across the bed and reached for the nightstand. My fingertips grazed the cool, wet glass but failed to grasp the bottle. I undid my binds, swung my feet out of the bed, planted them on the floor, and tried to stand. My balance had remained dormant on the bed, and I flailed and went crashing, face first, to the floor.

My hands did not react quickly enough—or had not wanted to react quickly enough—and it was my nose that took the brunt of the impact. Bone shattered and blood sprayed, then my teeth smacked the wood floor and rammed back into their gums. The jolt of pain was extreme, but it only lasted an instant. Unconsciousness ripped me away and cradled me in its dark embrace.

I must have been out several hours; though unconsciousness left no log of our communion; the blood around my nose and mouth and the blood puddled on my chest had coagulated. I lay in bed with no recollection of how I had got there, and my eyes immediately darted to the nightstand with the fear that they would find there some evidence of another horrible betrayal.

The bottle appeared to still be full. I righted myself and leaned over, lifted the bottle, and took a sip. It was not my intent. My intent had only been investigation, yet I could not stop, nor did I try to stop my hand and my mouth. Once the first drop hit my parched throat, I poured until the liquid had filled me and overflowed down my chin and my cheeks. Only when I had emptied the bottle of its contents did I come to the realization that it was, in fact, merely water. I collapsed onto the bed, relieved yet still in a state of disbelief. Had I given the demon too much credit? Had I not given myself enough?

My memory played for me, again, the images of me filling up the beer bottle at the kitchen sink. I rejoiced, and I apologized to my memory for the scepticism—albeit well-warranted scepticism: a point I did not fail to bring up in my defence.

It was in this joyous reconciliation that I had a second realization: my legs were no longer bound by the curtains I'd tied them up with. I shifted them freely in disbelief. Then I tore off the covers, which served to let out and fan the stench of liquid faeces, urine, blood, and sweat. The odour attacked my nostrils and rattled my head. I felt another heave come on, but I fought it back; my stomach was too sore for such exertion.

The stench was a new obstacle, one I had not prepared for—in the past, Jonathon had always been there to clean up for me. I had to prioritize my efforts between stopping the room from spinning and avoiding another heave. I failed at both.

A violent wave of peristalsis grabbed everything it could—intestines, liver, kidneys, bowels—and yanked them and tried to stuff them up my oesophagus only to let go at the last moment so they'd flop and bounce around my empty stomach.

I then had to fight off another fainting spell.

I failed at that, too.

***

'Jonathon, this time will be different. I promise. You believe me, don't you?'

'Jonathon?'

'Don't look at me like that, Jonathon.' His eyes stayed fast on me. I turned to the left; there they awaited me. I turned to the right; there they greeted me.

'I'm going to do what needs to be done. I'll never again drink. I'll never again smoke. I'll never again inject or digest another drug. Look me in me eyes and tell me you don't believe me.'

I felt his eyes bore into mine, hot at first, then scalding. I blinked, and his gaze was still upon me. I scratched and clawed at my eyes till the vision exploded into a splatter of reds.

'I believe you, Michael.' I could hear hope in his voice, but not conviction.

'Say it again, Jonathon.'

'I believe you, Michael.' Identical, as if a broken record, static and with the audible skip of the needle. 'I believe you, Michael.'

I swung my arms violently, yet there was no record player to hit, to knock out of commission. The line repeated. 'I believe you, Michael.'

I scratched and clawed at my ears till the voice turned into a more pleasant siren.

'I do believe you, Michael.' His thoughts had commandeered my thoughts. 'I must go now. Come for me. I still love you.'

Those words gripped me, paralyzed me. Jonathon had never been able to say he loved me. 'A lie! All a lie!'

Of course it was. *I am a rational man. I know that Jonathon cannot communicate with me telepathically. We were hardly able to communicate when we were in the same room, much less the hundreds of miles that must separate us now.*

I dug my nails into my thighs as punishment. How had I nearly fallen for such a pathetic ruse!? Having exhausted physical torture, hunger, and thirst, the demon was now trying an emotional ploy. *I am not unsympathetic, but does it assume me so stupid!?*

I calmed myself and deduced that it was no underestimation on the demon's part. It simply had no other arms to use. Would it now try for pity? Would it make an appeal to my heart? Beg for compassion?

I resolved to turn a deaf ear to any such attempt. My heart was hardened; I would accept no apology.

I lay in bed, in my own filth, and waited for a final twitch or a final craving to come calling. So weakened was I from the days' battle that I felt the strong pull of gravity as if trying to suck me through the bed. At the same time, there was a lightness to my being, as if every fibre of me, every individual molecule were being lifted by delicate threads. Soon I would flutter away; soon I would dissolve into nothing.

I propped myself up on my elbows. I'd need to shower, retrieve the key, and venture outside a new man, a hungry and feeble man, but one who was in control of his own body, battered and broken as it may be.

My decision was made, but the strength to carry it out had not yet come to me when, instead of sitting up, I witnessed a form leave my body, stand up, and wobble before falling to the floor. The line between memory and the moment ceased to exist, or at least I no longer distinguished it. Yet when I patted my hands around me, they found soft, soiled sheets and not a hardwood floor.

The confusion was nauseating. What had I witnessed? The past? A formerly locked-up memory only now surfacing and intruding upon my present reality? The nausea was a storm in my belly. Simmering acids popped just under the skin, searing the flesh, leaving tiny blemishes of black and blue.

I turned my head to heave, and the air and the acids expunged from my belly caught in my throat. There on the floor beside my bed, I saw him—or 'it', I should say. It lay face down, hands outstretched on either side. At first glance, it did look like me. But upon further examination, its pallid skin and spidering blue veins betrayed the illusion. I reached down to touch it, and it moved. I turned over with a jerk, back onto the bed, and fixed the ceiling with determined eyes: determined not to fall for its trick, determined to see that hideous thing that lay a foot away from me for what it truly was.

There comes a moment of 'clarity' when an addict accepts that he will always be an addict. 'You can't kill it. You can only learn to manage it,' was the mantra.

But that is not clarity; it is cowardice.

Of course you can kill it, if you dare.

If you expel it from your body through extreme deprivation and not feed it the poison it craves, it will lie on the floor beside you, exposed and vulnerable. I had often imagined this as a dream, but right then I knew it as a fact. I covered my eyes, for fear the image would be too unsettling or perhaps, in its sad state, too sympathetic, and I leaned over the bed, peering through the cracks in my fingers. Amid the dancing spots of fiery reds and popping yellows, beyond the veil of my watery and bloody eyes, I saw it. I stared at it. I contemplated it.

Now it lay on its back, its face with skin stretched taught as if at any moment it would snap, its eyes pulpous gashes leaking fluids that streamed down its hollowed cheeks. Beyond the grotesque nature of its appearance, there was a likeness to my own that did not leave me indifferent. I summoned what little strength I still possessed and leaned over, my hand extended.

I touched a demon on the cheek. It quivered under my trembling fingertips. I felt a cold shock rush through my body, and I quivered in return.

Its eyes searched me and found me. They implored me, yet I was resolute, and I shook my head.

I swung my legs out of bed and set them on the cold hardwood floor. I took a moment to gather my strength. In that moment, the demon rose. It turned its head from me and lumbered toward the door.

I did not need to summon any strength—for the demon still had a pull on me, one I did not resist. As if tethered—I knew, in fact, that I was still tethered—my steps imitated its steps, pained and sluggish.

I followed it through the door and into the bathroom. When it reached the sink, it turned its head to me. Its eyes no longer red and gouged but rather young and afraid. The illusion was but a flicker, and it was gone. Yet behind the tears of blood, the fear remained.

I, too, was afraid, and I extended a trembling hand.

I touched a demon on the cheek. Its eyelids drifted shut. The corners of its mouth floated upwards. Its face conformed to the crook of my palm and cradled itself therein. It started to speak, but I breathed a 'shhh'; and its aborted plea brushed my wrist, tickling it as would a feather.

The demon had a frail frame, wrapped grotesquely in twisted and torn flesh. Splotches of black, blue, and grey speckled its arms and torso. Its bony legs ended in swollen feet, one twisted to point unnaturally to the side.

As I examined this hideous creature before me—the cause of so much pain and destruction—I did feel a touch of sympathy: sympathy I had foreseen and prepared for. I remained steadfast in my resolution, steadfast and now steady-handed.

The demon—for it was a demon, something horrific birthed from fear and despair—turned from me to face the mirror and gazed upon its naked self. It tried to imitate me, but it wasn't me. It tried to contort its features to resemble mine, but I was not fooled.

I looked into the mirror, and from an angle, I found its eyes. Amid the cuts and abrasions, its pupils stared back at me. I, though repulsed, did not turn away. 'It ends here,' I said.

It shook its head.

'It ends here,' I repeated.

It raised an arm, not at me but toward the medicine cabinet. I slid behind the demon while it pulled out a bottle of pain killers. It closed the cabinet, and our faces superimposed in the mirror's reflection. With slow motions it opened the cap to the bottle, but I took it from its hand. It grabbed my wrist, but its grip was weak. It could but watch as I poured the pills down the drain. A pair of scissors lay in the basin. It saved two of the pills from sliding down the dark hole. I lifted the scissors and, with their point, gave the pills a little flick, and they were gone.

'It ends here,' I repeated.

The demon's lips parted. A desperate and breathy 'no' escaped.

I transferred the scissors from my left hand to my right. With my left hand, I reached up and clutched the demon by its jaw.

It tried to speak once more, but it was weak and I was strong.

'I won't lie,' I said. And not without a bit of pleasure, I added, 'but this is going to hurt.'

I opened the scissors and slid the blades around the demon's right ear. 'With this ear you had me hear things that were not true.'

It tried to squirm free, but it was weak and I was strong.

I snipped. The flesh was tough and would not easily tear. I squeezed hard on the scissors and cut and pulled until the bloody ear came off and fell into the sink.

The demon screamed a scream so loud and pained that even my own throat could feel it.

'With these lips, you deceived and you made promises you never intended to keep,' I said as I closed the scissors around the demon's lower lip.

The demon tried to squirm free from my clutches, but it was weak and I was strong.

I cut, and the lip fell from the face like bulbous fat off a tender cut of meat. Blood flowed down its chin and trickled onto the sink's white porcelain border. The demon mouthed a 'no' which splattered the mirror.

'Yes,' I replied, and I cut off its upper lip.

The demon's knees buckled, but my grip did not loosen. I held it up, forced it to stand, and rammed the scissors into the demon's cheek. I punctured the skin and yanked, slicing all the way back to the demon's lying mouth.

The demon could no longer stand. I bent it over the sink and stabbed it in its side. In its ribs. In its thigh. I stabbed and stabbed until all my strength was exhausted and I crumpled to the floor.

I laboured to keep my eyes from closing, and I searched for signs of the demon.

The demon was dead; I had killed him, and his body had vanished.

I laid my head against the cold tile floor and listened to drops of blood splash into puddles near my mouth and at my sides. The pitter patter sounded off the walls and the floor, then the reverberations carried down the corridor and into the living room.

As I lay there and listened, the blood began to drip less incesantly from the sink, yet the tapping sound persisted in the living room, heavier like slow padded footfalls.

'Jonathon,' I called out.

'Jonathon, I've made another mess.'

AND THEN CAME THE SLUGS

Tears welled in my eyes—not from the pain, though I did indeed feel pain—but from the acrid air thick with the stench of sweat and stale whiskey excreting out of the brute's scum-crusted pores. The sight of my suffering always did bring him pleasure, so I wiped my eyes dry and put on a cold, stern face. I wasn't going to give him the satisfaction.

Though he stood on the other side of the room—a good five or six paces from me—I could still smell the rot of each laboured breath he took. Panting like a sickly dog, his chest heaved and his bloated belly pushed against the confines of his overstretched trousers whose fibres clung to one another on the brink of rupture. I kept my eyes on him; I did not turn away, my fear superseded by sheer fascination. How grotesque, how unspeakably horrific: his face, reddened and glistening from the sudden physical exertion, his hair matted in greasy clumps to his shining forehead, his eyes, sunk deep in their orbits, piercing the shadows to glare at me with dilated pupils glossed over with rage.

I put a hand to my cheek where he had struck me, conscious to avoid trembling—if he couldn't, through his own stink, smell the fear in me, I wouldn't let him see it. My skin was hot to the touch, surprisingly hot, the nerve endings panicked and rushing fevered sensations to my already agitated mind. The jaw bone underneath was soft and gave to the light pressure of my fingers. My teeth, loosened from the blow, threatened to fall from the slackened hold of my sore gums.

'Is it broken?' he asked.

The list of things that were broken was long and had been counted and recounted many times over in the last year: trust, dignity, hope, dreams, happiness. Funny he should care about something as insignificant as my bones. I wiggled my jaw; it would be fine. Through the pain, I gritted my teeth. 'You shouldn't have hit me,' I said.

He spat out a breath of laughter and glanced reflexively at his hand. I discerned a gleam of pleasure flash in his eyes. 'You shouldn't have provoked me,' he said.

He stepped away from the wall, out of the shadow. The light did not flatter him. The bottom button of his shirt was unfastened, exposing a portion of his bulbous belly. It jiggled with his breaths, the fat moving in ripples as if it were but a layer of skin covering a nest of squirming larvae; that if I were to get hold of a knife and slice him open, his belly would spew forth a torrent of little writhing things to the floor.

He cracked his neck and then his knuckles. 'Always provoking me, when all I want to do is come home from a hard day at the factory, have a decent meal waiting for me, and enjoy a little peace and quiet. Is that too much to ask?'

I wondered, in turn, if it wasn't too much to ask that his breath not reek of dead fish, if it wasn't too much to ask for the floor to give in under his weight and that he fall through and that one of the splintered floorboards should slice through his over-fed belly and come out his flabby neck and that a geyser of blood would jet from the wide and painful puncture. I wondered: is that too much to ask?

I made no attempt to stifle the smile forming on my face.

'Something funny?' he asked.

I didn't answer. He wouldn't have seen the humour in it anyway.

He did not insist on a reply. Instead, he walked past me, hovering over me a second as he did so. With each plodding step, his belly shook, and a second bottom button of his shirt snapped. I had to chuckle.

'Soon your bulbous belly will burst free and flop onto the floor,' I said. 'Then the pod of slugs nesting in your stomach will awake and gnaw their way out.'

He glared at me and through gritted tobacco-stained teeth said, 'The pod of—What the hell are you on about?'

'And don't think I'm going to clean it up!' I said.

He raised his hand at me, open palmed, a brute's swipe away from my other cheek. 'What did you say?'

'I said, 'the pod of slugs nesting in your sto—'

He slapped me and exited the room.

I had more to say—more on critter eggs hatching in his bowels then the swarm of beetles and bugs scurrying through his stomach, their tiny feet catching on his intestines and pulling them out with them as they squeezed their way through the gash of torn flesh in his overstretched belly—but all that pretty poetry went unvoiced. Instead, I stood from the sofa in silence and followed him down the hall.

He slipped into the bathroom yet left the door open. And as he ran his hands under the faucet, he looked up and caught my reflection in the bathroom mirror. At the doorway, at arm's length, head up, shoulders back, I stared at him.

He grinned, splashed water on his face then turned to me. 'What do you want?'

I wanted many things: the obvious, that he should cease breathing; that the stench of sweat and alcohol he emitted be replaced by the rust-like tang of his blood; that his bloated belly be ripped open and all the squirming things inside fall to the ground so that I may stomp on them and squish them under the heel of my shoe. I wanted the last year of my life back. I wanted my dreams back, my happiness, my dignity.

In response to his question, I stated something far less ambitious though equally inadmissible and enraging to his ears. 'I want an apology.'

He shook his wet hands in the air. The pupils of his blackened eyes contracted, and I was reminded of a snake coiling and arching back before its attack. He stepped toward me. His mouth opened. Yet before words could escape the pit of rot they'd been summoned from, his hand darted through the air and caught my neck. 'An apology! Are you fucking crazy!?'

His thumb and index finger bore into my neck. I could not breathe. He pinned my back against the door; the doorknob dug into the base of my spine. Instantly, I lost all sensation in my legs, and though I wanted my hands to grab his hand and pry the fingers from their grip, my arms hung inert at my sides.

'You want an apology!' he barked, spittle spraying my face. 'Here's your fucking apology!'

And with that promise, he eased his grip on my neck so that my feet may grace the floor, then he grabbed me by my shirt, balling the front of it into his fist, dragged me down the hallway, and hurled me across the living room.

My head narrowly missed the corner of the table. My back smacked against the chair, and I crumpled to the floor.

I may have survived the attack—I had survived similar ones before. Or I may very well have died right there and then; the difference between death and survival, for me, was a question of mere semantics at that point. Perhaps it was the gentle hand of death that closed my eyelids and wrapped me in a cold veil of darkness. I didn't feel any pain—at least none that I can remember; I don't remember losing consciousness, either. I only remember the violence and the fear, the dream of slit bellies and slimy slugs.

And then the nightmare began.

***

At first, I thought the knocking was coming from inside my head, but the voice of my loyal friend (clearly from the corridor outside my flat) disabused me of that delusion.

'Are you there? I hope you haven't forgotten our plans,' she said.

I made a move to pull myself off the floor—*What am I doing on the floor?*—and a searing pain shot through my body. I loosed a cry and collapsed.

My body had been infiltrated—though I couldn't say when. Steel claws had found their way in, somehow, and they had dug into my spine. Presently, they stretched and pulled and tugged as if wanting to disassemble my vertebrae one molecule at a time. Fire shot out from my lower back in rhythm with my quickening heartbeat.

'I can't get up,' I yelled. 'Help me.'

My loyal friend rattled the doorknob then kicked the door.

'The good neighbour to the right has a key,' I called out.

Moments later, my loyal friend opened the door, and with the good neighbour trailing behind her, they entered my home, found me sprawled on the floor, and rushed over to my aid.

I cried, from the pain of course but also out of fear. I couldn't move my legs and thought I might be paralyzed. Yet, after some effort, I was able to wiggle my left foot. Oh the joy at that moment in seeing my left foot obey my command. It is the simple things in life, sometimes, that bring us the most pleasure.

My loyal friend tried to help me up, but the pain was too great. I cried, and I clung to the floor. The good neighbour placed a pillow under my head so that I may lay in relative comfort, and he called a doctor.

Despite my pleas and my protests, the three of them, my loyal friend, the good neighbour, and the doctor, lifted me from the floor and laid me on the sofa. The pain I suffered was so intense and had spread to such an extent that I was unable to detect its original source. My stomach, my bowels, my back, my legs: all seemed plausible and perfectly reasonable culprits. Since I did not wish to share how the pain had come on and what had led to my being sprawled on the floor, the doctor had his own pains in diagnosing me.

'We will get you something for the pain,' said the doctor. 'For now, just lie down and try to relax. If you are not better tomorrow, you'll come to the clinic for some tests.'

Tomorrow I will be dead, I thought. But that was just wishful thinking.

The good neighbour fetched pain medicine from the chemist's then left me in the company and care of my loyal friend. She told me to be strong, that the pain medicine would soon kick in, that it was of the highest potency, and that everything would turn out OK. I told her about the slugs in the brute's belly and how I would slice him open and how they would flop to the floor where I would crush them under the heel of my shoe.

Oh, how we laughed.

She told me of a recent case she'd read about, of travelers who had eaten some questionable food and then returned home harbouring a colony of bugs, worms, and parasites in their stomachs. The worms and such ate away at all their fat and muscle untill they were left with mere skin and bones. But besides that, they were perfectly healthy. She said that perhaps bugs and worms and parasites would do the obese brute some good.

Oh, how we laughed.

My loyal friend then offered to go out and buy groceries. 'You just lie here and rest. I'll fill up the fridge and the cupboards. You need not worry about that,' she said.

'And don't forget to pick up some bugs and worms and parasites,' I said, and I think I smiled, though I had no feeling in my face, so I couldn't be sure.

No sooner had she returned and had put away her purchases than the brute returned from the factory.

From the doorway, he stared at the two of us before entering.

My loyal friend greeted him with an up-beat 'hello' and proceeded to inform him about the state she had found me in and the actions she and the good neighbour had taken. He, in brute fashion, merely grunted, slammed the door shut, and plodded down the hallway across the living room and into the kitchen.

I gave him no greeting; I said nothing and didn't even glance his way. My loyal friend rubbed her legs nervously and glanced around for something inoffensive to occupy her attention.

The refrigerator opened and closed, then the brute plodded back into the living room. He stood there, in a place not too far from where he'd started his aggression the previous night, a beer in one hand, the other hand on his hip, a scowl on his face. 'So, you've just been lying there all day, then?'

My loyal friend answered for me, or she attempted to. 'Well, um, of course she has. The doctor—'

'I'd like to lie on the sofa all day, watching TV,' he interrupted. 'Maybe my back hurts too.' He took a swig of his beer. 'But no. Someone has to pay the rent.'

I turned, not without difficulty, to my loyal friend. 'Thank you so much for keeping me company. You'd better go now.'

With the brute not having moved, still looming over us, albeit from across the room, my loyal friend dropped her voice to a whisper. 'Are you sure?'

I mustered what I could of a smile. 'Yes, I'm sure.'

'Everything you need is in the fridge and in the cupboards.' She winked at me and patted my hand. 'I'll come by tomorrow afternoon. Check in on you.' She offered the brute a nervous half wave and scurried out of the flat.

I went back to watching the TV where a bubbly woman in a bright red sweater had just won 25,000 euros. She jumped for joy, and her husband rushed the stage to take her in his arms and spin her around, smiling and kissing her cheek.

'I'm hungry,' said the brute.

***

Over the following weeks, with my loyal friend's help, I saw as many doctors as I had ailments. Each failed to find the root cause of my woes, preferring, instead, to dispatch me with unreadable prescriptions I'd then exchange at the chemist's for unpronounceable pharmaceuticals. By the end of the month, I had amassed quite the collection of medication. I had a white pill for the nausea in my stomach; a blue one for the poor circulation troubling my legs; off-yellow for my headaches; bright-yellow for joint pains. And each pill had its side effects which required another pill to counteract. My breakfast was a veritable cornucopia of coloured tablets. By lunchtime, I was relieving myself in rainbows.

The brute was not any less brutish over that time. Fortunately, my mind was, more often than not, so clouded and distant that his insults, threats, and accusations failed to inflict the hurt they were intended to. Besides, no pain he'd promise could rival that which my own body was meting out to me on a constant basis.

Though I had but a flimsy grasp on consciousness over that time, I was keenly aware—and quite pleasantly so—of the brute's growing frustrations. No longer would his dutiful wife have a hot meal prepared for him upon his return from the factory. No longer could she carry on the simplest of conversations with him or even feign to pay attention to his ramblings. And though his frustrations mounted, he could no longer rid himself of them through fist and fury—for what fury could be unleashed upon this semi-conscious heap of flesh I'd become, nearly inert and surely inoffensive lying on the sofa? Of course he kicked a boot through the TV screen. It did little to calm his anger, though it may have improved my viewing experience. He smashed a few plates and punched the occasional hole in the wall. But what did it matter? I was in no shape to clean up the pieces or care much about the damage to something as trivial as my home.

His frustrations grew to such an extent that after a few weeks he took on a second shift at the factory, preferring to pound away at metal with the factory's many heavy machines than to mope about the flat complaining about what he deserved from a wife and what his, in this cruel reality, was unable to give him.

I saw less and less of the brute, though his presence nevertheless lingered. The foul stench of sweat and liquor emitted from his body clung to the air well after he'd left for the day. A draught from some unknown source would cause it to stir, as if he were storming through the flat, passing by me in a rush only to return and hover above me. The ugliest of the words he'd spit out in his drunken diatribes would reverberate in the room. They'd gather in the crevices and fissures of the walls; they'd hide in the bookshelves and under the sofa and wait till he'd leave before coming out to swarm and buzz about my ears.

When he was home, I was under constant threat: he was capable of coming for me at any moment. When he was away, I was under constant threat: he was capable of returning to me at any moment. I said to my loyal friend, 'I haven't slept in days. How is it possible, then, that I could have so many nightmares?'

My loyal friend brewed for me herbal teas and brought for me pills. She stocked the refirgerator and the cupboards. 'Soon the nightmare will end,' she said.

I don't know exactly why; perhaps it was the sly smile on her face or the knowing wink she gave me, but I believed her.

***

'Look at you,' the brute spat out with disdain. 'You lie on the sofa day and night half out of your wits. And me, I slave away in a hot factory! You sleep like a log. And I'm lucky if I can get more than a few hours of shut-eye before it's back to the factory and back to the machines.'

'Why, then, don't you just crawl into one of those machines and go to sleep?' I responded.

'Stupid woman,' he said. 'The machines are made for cutting and forging metals and alloys. They're not made for sleeping in!'

'What's the worst that could happen?' I asked. 'You'd be crushed or chopped up by a machine? Doesn't the factory have a cleaning crew?'

The brute stomped across the room. He hovered over me—or perhaps it was only the stench of him that took form and hovered over me; I didn't turn my head to get a good look. I did, however, hear him snatch one of my bottles of pills from the corner table. 'Lying on the sofa all day popping pills. And just listen to you!' He hurled the bottle across the room. It smacked against the wall. The cap popped off, and a beautiful cascade of sky-blue pills rained down onto the table. The sound was like hail against a windshield, and I was reminded of the time we had driven across the country during a storm. But then I remembered that was only one of the stories my loyal friend had told me just the day prior and we had never actually driven anywhere, neither in good weather nor in a storm. It was getting hard to tell the difference between memories of the stories my loyal friend would tell me and memories of the life I had lived. And I was thankful for that gentle mercy.

The brute would come home at all hours of the night in all states of inebriation; that much had remained constant. Fortunately, I was no longer forced to share his bed. And though the bedroom was at the opposite end of the flat, I could still hear his loud, thunderous snoring and sniffles and grunts. Some mornings, upon waking, he would force me up, lift me, literally, carry me into the kitchen, and set me before the stove. Searing pain would shoot from my back, run down my legs, and twist and squeeze at every muscle. It was impossible for me to stand, so I'd crumple to the floor. The brute would pull me up by my hair and sit me on a stool. 'I've got to work day and night down at the factory,' he'd bark. 'The least you could do is make me breakfast. Eggs, bacon, beans, ham, and toast.'

I'd be too dizzy and disoriented to cook, of course. On one occasion, I burnt the eggs and forgot to take the bacon out of the wrapper before putting it in the frying pan. The meat I tossed in the skillet was doubtfully ham and undoubtedly not the colour good meat should have. What did I care? Or what did the brute care, for that matter? What's a few more larvae and bacteria to add to the collection nesting in his stomach? I tossed whatever I could find in the frying pan—what I found in the cupboards might have been beans, I wasn't sure or interested in being sure—and I smothered it all with butter and cooked until the foul stench made me pass out.

The brute wouldn't leave me any peace. Instead, he slapped me around until I was again burdened with consciousness. He claimed the slop I'd whipped up was the most vile, most inedible thing one could concoct, then he proceeded to eat it all up greedily.

Over the weeks, while I withered away for want of appetite, the brute put on considerable pounds. On the rare occasions I would be awake and somewhat alert and he would be home, I would catch a glimpse of him lumbering across the living room to fetch himself a cold beer from the fridge, shirtless, his harry blob-like belly hanging over his punished waistline. The flabby pockets of his flesh seemed to move independently of his plodding steps. I would see them in my waking dreams: bubbling, gelatinous globs of sweat- and grime-smeared flesh, moving, plodding across the room. A hive of bees would not have agitated as much. I dreamt frequently of popping his belly open like a piñata and thus releasing a cloud of buzzing bees that would swarm his face and fly by the thousands into his mouth when he'd open it to scream.

I dreamt often of bees.

But that was before the slugs.

***

The brute was multiplying double shifts at the factory. And, in consequence, his sleep did suffer. And, in consequence, so did his vigilance and care at work. It was, I remember it well, a glorious springtime morning; the sun was shining; the birds were singing; and the brute came home early with bandages around his hand and eyes glazed from things I knew all too well: pain and fear and tears.

He stormed right up to me on the sofa. He shoved his bandaged hand right up to my face. It smelled of disinfectant and rust. 'This is your fault!' he yelled. 'All your fault! All your doing!

'I work all day, all night, while you lie on the sofa popping pills,' he continued ranting, pacing the living room with his bandaged hand extended out in front of him as if he were addressing it in a loud theatrical voice that would surely carry to the back of the hall, 'and I can't get a decent night's sleep. Then it's back to the factory. And look at this!' He lunged, bringing once again his mutilated hand into my face for me to behold.

The sight was grotesque: three digits pointed up and a stump where the index finger should have been. Though as grotesque as the sight was, my attention was diverted toward his belly, for the shirt he was wearing was too tight, and between two of its buttons with the fabric stretched apart, I could garner a peek at his belly—only a slight, tiny glimpse. But it was enough for me to see the ripple of activity underneath.

He grabbed my jaw and squeezed, the stumped index finger wiggling and feeling for my bottom lip. 'What do you have to say for yourself?' yelled the brute.

'I don't think your belly is full of bees,' I said, 'but full of something thicker and slower in movement: fat worms possibly, but most likely slugs.'

'Crazy woman!' The brute took my pill bottles from the table beside the sofa, and he hurled them across the room. They scattered about the floor on the other side of the living room.

Later that night as the brute snored in his comfortable bed at the other end of the flat, when the pain and the nausea and the dizziness rose to insupportable heights, I pulled myself off the sofa, crumpled to the floor, and dragged my limp body across the room toward the scattered pills.

The floorboards quivered beneath my hands; in some places where the boards were the loosest, they shook and rattled. I crawled ever the more quickly for fear that whatever was alive and agitating underneath should break free of its confines and assault my defenceless body. When I'd finally reached the pills and ingested a healthy amount, I lay down on the floor and rested before I would have to embark on a painful and laborious struggle back to the sofa. With my ear to the floor, I could hear them squirming and wiggling and nibbling and struggling to come out.

At the base of the wall, something pushed against the skirting boards, and they appeared to bubble like simmering milk. *It is only a matter of time,* I thought, *till they break free. I shall be covered with slimy, creepy crawly things. God help me.*

So ripe was my fear of whatever was simmering under the floorboards that it took precedence over the excruciating pain in my back and legs, and very quickly did I manage to crawl back to the sofa and pull myself onto it. Needless to say, I got not a moment's sleep that night, staring vigilantly at the skirts and the floorboards, awaiting their inevitable breach.

When the brute awoke to take his hasty breakfast in the living room, the floors ceased their simmering. *Whatever's agitating underneath seems to be quelled by his presence,* I thought. Yet I was disabused of this notion once he left and the stirring did not begin anew.

The scene repeated itself the following night as well. I surmised, then, that these slimy, creepy crawly things under the floorboards must be of a nocturnal nature.

Yet again, I could not, would not shut my eyes and give in to the siren's call of sleep. Only when my loyal friend came round in the afternoon to keep me company did I manage a bit of rest. She started to tell me a tale—or perhaps I dreamt she did—a tale of catapillars and butterflies and cataflies and butterpillars. They would weave cocoons as small as grains of salt and speckle the leaves of a mint plant like morning frost. Before she could finish her tale, the brute returned, staggering drunk and smelling of liquor, sweat, and grease.

'Do you see what she's done to me?' He shouted at my loyal friend and showed her his bandaged hand of three fingers, a thumb, and a stump.

'Let her be,' I said.

He pointed his stump at me and said, 'I'm in MY home. Don't you—' A mucous-laden belch cut him off. He winced, grabbed his grumbling belly, and plopped down in a chair.

'You'd better go,' I said to my loyal friend.

She did not protest but promised to return the following afternoon.

Lest she linger over the goodbyes, the brute relieved himself of pent-up gases. The room filled with the stench of rot and excrement and hydrogen sulphide. Both I and my loyal friend curled our noses and covered our faces. The brute laughed and bid my loyal friend a safe return home. Once the door had closed behind her, the brute turned to me; all traces of any laugh vanished from his face.

'How long are you going to lie there useless and moping on that sofa?'

'Until I get well.'

'You will never get well. You were never well to begin with.' He came at me with his bandaged hand. His stomach revolted from the effort. He grabbed his belly and belched. 'You're a sick, useless woman, and you're making me sick!'

'I can see you are sick,' I said. 'I can smell it, too.'

He hurled a teacup against the wall. He smashed a saucer. When he could find nothing left to throw, he cursed and yelled and belched then staggered off to bed.

And then came the slugs.

***

With the passage of each night, the rippling of activity underneath the floor grew in intensity. How was I to get my much needed rest if at night the creepy crawly things squirmed under the floors and if at any moment of the day the brute threatened to return drunk and hurl at me objects and insults, or worse yet, shove that mangled, mutilated hand in my face? 'And you think you're suffering!' he would yell. 'Look at it! Smell it!' And on more than one occasion, he'd tried to ram his stumped digit in my mouth. 'Taste it! This is your doing, woman!'

I shared my fears with my loyal friend.

'I have just the thing you need,' she said.

And then—though how I hadn't noticed it before I cannot tell— she handed me the gift she had brought: a silver-stemmed crutch with a padded armrest wrapped in a neat green bow.

'Thank you. You are too kind.'

'For now, you will only use it to go to and from the kitchen and the bathroom. But soon you will be strong and we will take it out for a stroll in the park.'

'Yes, I'd like that,' I said as I tried out the crutch with a few steps across the living room.

My loyal friend put a hand on my shoulder, leaned in, and whispered in my ear. 'And if those slimy bugs get out, you will crush them with the end of the crutch.'

Her comment, and the playful tone it was delivered with, surprised me, but not as much as the knowing wink she added upon seeing the beffudled look on my face. 'It has many uses. It can even be a brute-swatter if weilded right.'

With the aid of the crutch, I accompanied my loyal friend to the door where I thanked her again and kissed her goodbye. However, as I already feared the brute's reaction— 'Who gave this to you? Why do you need a crutch? Your leg's not broken. You're just being lazy and dellusional.'—I hid the crutch in the closet and not without difficulty lumbered my way back to the sofa.

It wasn't long before I came to regret stashing away the crutch, for while the brute snored comfortably in his bed, I, lying on the sofa, witnessed a stream of slugs slither out from one of the skirting boards. At first, I thought it was a crack in the wall that had come to life, and I rejoiced in the manifest delusion. Yet, as I watched the 'crack' spread like a weed sprouting in the drywall, I began, sadly, to doubt my insanity.

I pulled myself off the sofa. My legs refused to support my weight, and I was, thus, obliged to crawl, or more precisely, to slither on my stomach, dragging myself across the floor to the skirting board on the far side of the room.

There were ten of them: long thin slimy black things with no discernible head or feet or back. They moved slowly and in a fluid motion, like raindrops sliding down a windshield. But these little critters moved upward and they left no trail in their wake. My instinct was to crush them, to find a paper towel and smash them right where they slithered and smear them against the wall. However, when I crawled to the kitchen and opened the cupboard, next to the paper towel was a Tupperware container, and a more refined idea came to mind. I collected these little slugs and put them in the refrigerator to show to my loyal friend the next day. I applied adhesive to the crack in the skirting board, without much conviction that it would hold, but as weak as I was, I could not hope to do any better.

By the time I'd made it back to the sofa, I thought I would die. Maybe I did. Maybe what I experienced thereafter was a sort of purgatory: a lonely place between states where I was called upon to undergo a painful, yet long overdue, purge.

My loyal friend came to me—though I don't remember her knocking or me letting her in—and she found me in quite a pitiful state. 'You had a troubled night, I can see,' she said.

Pain had taken complete control of my limbs; nausea had taken complete control of my stomach, and dizziness and confusion were now the sole occupants of my mind. I was forced out of my body. Yet, as I floated, hovering over that wretched shell, I willed it to speak.

My loyal friend took my hand in hers, and she laid an ear against my lips. 'What is it? What are you trying to say?'

Before I succumbed to unconsciousness, I managed to utter, 'The slugs are coming.'

***

My loyal friend served me tea. The scent of it was of a flowering field in the summer. I was a little girl kneeling in the grass. A bee came to me and set a drop of honey on my lips. 'Thank you,' I said. 'Thank you, kindly bee.'

'You're welcome,' said my loyal friend. 'Feeling better?'

'Much better,' I surprised myself to hear. And it was true. I could move my legs without complaint from them, and the room merely swayed gently back and forth as opposed to the habitual whirlwind it had been of late. 'I feel so good I think I will get up, use the crutch, and maybe go outside for a walk.'

My loyal friend beamed. 'How wonderful to hear you say that. But finish your tea first. We are in no rush.'

She was right, and I told her so. I finished my tea and listened to her stories. Then I remembered the slugs. I sat up, set my legs on the floor, waited a beat for the room to steady, then I said, 'I have something to show you.'

'Oh?'

'The slugs,' I said. 'They've started to come.'

My loyal friend was visibly elated with the turn in conversation. 'The slugs, already?'

'Help me to the kitchen and I will show you.'

My loyal friend helped me up, and not a moment later, as if he'd been waiting at the door this whole time for his cue, in stormed the brute. 'Well, it's a miracle,' he proclaimed sarcastically. 'The lazy-ass woman is off the sofa.'

'I'm feeling slightly better, thank you,' I said.

'Good. Whip me up something to eat. I'm hungry.'

My loyal friend offered to make us both something, but I would not have her cooking for the brute; I wouldn't hear of it. 'You're a dear friend,' I told her, 'and you are an incredible help and comfort. But there are some things, as horrific as they are, that I must do myself.'

'You really shouldn't,' she replied, and I wondered if we were talking about the same thing.

'I will see you tomorrow,' I said, partly as a question, partly as a promise, but mostly as a mantra: one that I clung to for hope and for comfort.

'I will see you tomorrow,' she said, and she kissed me on the forehead and was gone.

'I hear a lot of blabbing and not a lot of cooking,' bellowed the brute from the living room. Already, the stench of him had made its way into the kitchen; already, my stomach was in revolt, and I was weak and had to cling to the counter for support.

'Do I need to come in there?' The brute stood at the doorway. 'Do you need a hand?' He thrust his mangled extremity in my face, wiggling his stumped digit around in search of my mouth. He laughed at me as, with my bout of dizziness, I struggled to stay standing while trying to prevent my face from coming into contact with that smelly bandaged stump. He laughed so hard his belly bounced and jiggled, waking the legion of larvae therein, making his flabby flesh ripple with their agitation.

He winced and put his mangled hand to his belly. 'Hurry up, will you?' he said. 'I'm so hungry it hurts.'

I had no empathy for the brute, of course. I had no strength to cook, either. But to avoid a scene, I summoned enough determination, and I did the best I could. I emptied containers of things I found in the refrigerator into a pot of boiling water. I called it soup, served him a bowl, and collapsed on the sofa.

'Worthless woman!' yelled the brute. 'Even the slop down at the factory is better than this.' Nevertheless, he ate, and slurped, and belched.

***

Things scurried and slithered underneath me. A stench of rot wafted up from them, so strong it stung my eyes. The brute tapped my cheek, waking me from my nightmare and into another. 'Get up and do some housework,' he said. 'This place is a mess.' He parted with threats of returning later.

And I did get up; and I did get to work.

I pulled myself off the sofa and, with the help of my crutch, lumbered all the way to the back room, to the closet where we kept tools for various purposes. Therein I found a hammer and several screwdrivers of different heads and thicknesses.

I went back to the living room with the intention of ripping up the floorboards, or at least rip up one floorboard, and kill the slugs nesting underneath. The searing pain in my back and the nausea and the dizziness were relegated to distant concerns as I scoured the floor for a small crack or crevasse I could fit the head of a screwdriver into. I found more than one, which did provoke in me quite a panic. *If I don't find them and kill them now while they sleep, surely they will break through these tiny cracks at night and they will come out by the thousands and overtake me.*

Fear and the panic fuelled my resolve. I jammed the screwdriver into a crack, struck it with the hammer, and pried and pulled. But the floorboard did not come loose. *I'm only making things worse!*

One floorboard, however,—the one closest to the hallway—did loosen at my efforts. The exhilaration of such an important task nearing its completion was better medicine to my aching body than any of the coloured pills I'd been consuming. So elated was I and eager to complete the task that I failed to hear the front door open and close. And just as I had loosened the board to the point where a few more strategically placed strikes from my tools would rip it from its hold, my loyal friend put an arm around me and pulled me back. 'What on earth are you doing?'

'My loyal friend,' I said, 'I need your help to remove this floorboard.'

She shook her head, crouched down next to me, and attempted to lift me from the floor. 'Let's get you back to the sofa. You shouldn't be exerting yourself like this.'

I didn't have the strength to resist her. 'I have to get them when they're asleep. You don't understand, at night they come for me. Soon they will get me.'

My loyal friend gave me water and put a damp cloth on my head. 'My poor dear, you have a fever.'

'No, I don't,' I protested.

'You're burning up.'

'That's only from the effort, from the work I was doing. Those boards are laid good and tight.'

'My poor dear.' She could not be persuaded. 'Rest,' she said, 'and when you are better, I have something special for you.'

The 'something special' I wanted, the 'something special' I had so strongly wished for, was for the floorboards to be removed, the slugs to be crushed, and the brute to be dismembered and disembowelled by the machines down at the factory; now that they'd had a taste of his finger, let them finish the job.

My loyal friend, however, had a different sort of 'something special' for me: strawberries covered in chocolate.

'You are kind,' I said. 'They will not keep the slugs away, but they are delicious.'

'The slugs will not get you,' said my loyal friend. And with the conviction and sincerity in her words, I believed her. 'Soon you will have all your strength back and everything will be all right.' She gave me a pill—one I suspected was for the pain, but not long thereafter I was fast asleep.

I had not slept so profoundly perhaps in all my life—certainly not in any recent weeks. As my sleep was deep so were my dreams vivid.

Surrounded by black—but not a black of nothing; there was something in that blackness, something I could not see yet could feel, thick and heavy and approaching me from all sides—before me, at my feet, the floorboards stretched out, rippling with activity. The brute was there, of course. Why should sleep accord me any respite from his torment? He stood far away, shirtless. And despite the distance, every fold of his flabby flesh was visible to me. They, too, rippled with activity, seemingly synchronised with that of the floorboards in a grotesque dance of squiggly, protruding lines and bubbling dots.

He reached out to me with his bandaged mutilated hand. And as he did so, his arm expanded, stretching to cover the vast distance separating us. I had my crutch with me. I planted it on the floor, but it sunk as if swallowed by the boards. And from the base of the crutch, grey and black slugs began to climb.

I ripped my eyes from the horror and scanned my surroundings for an exit. There was but an all-consuming blackness around me. And coming my way, the hand, the endlessly stretching hand. Despite myself, I opened my mouth to scream. Before the cry could escape my lungs, the hand was upon me. The stumped index finger wriggled its way loose of the bandage, not unlike the slugs climbing the crutch. It found my mouth and slid over my tongue to the back of my throat, stifling the scream. I gagged; I was suffocating, unable to yell out, unable to breathe, and yet the arm kept stretching, and the stumped index finger kept squirming its way down my throat.

'I work all day at the factory!' It was not the brute who spoke, though it was his voice bellowing from the blackness, bellowing from all around me. 'I come home tired and hungry, and what do I get? A warm meal? A gentle word? A loving wife who will rub the soreness from my arms?'

A chorus of a hundred laughs, like the canned laughter of a TV sitcom, erupted from the darkness.

'No. I get a nagging, ungrateful wife who can't even get her lazy fat ass off the sofa!'

More canned laughter.

And the floorboards ripped open.

And then came the slugs.

With the brute's arm down my throat and his bandaged hand digging around in the pit of my stomach, I watched, helpless, as thousands of slugs moved on me, covering me with a thick glistening layer of slime.

Instead of their cold, wet touch, I felt the hard smack of the floor and woke from my horrors. I had managed, mercifully, in my sleep to throw myself off the sofa. Though I'd smacked my cheek on the floor and it did hurt, I was relieved to be able to take in a lungful of air. I greedily took in a second and a third and lay there on the floor gasping for breath and slapping my body in search of phantom slugs.

I do not know if my fall or my subsequent gasps awoke the brute or if it was yet another manifestation of bad timing that plagued me, but the brute, at that moment, plodded down the hallway in my direction.

He stopped at the threshold. With grimy nails he scratched at his naked belly as one would a purring cat.

'So, you've finally got your lazy fat ass off the sofa,' he said. 'Perfect timing. I'm hungry. Go make me breakfast.'

The morning sun fell bright in the living room, and my eyes could not as of yet fully open. I wanted desperately to reassure myself that the floorboards had not ripped open and that the slugs were not, as I lay, crawling toward me. My only recourse was to tatter my hands about, the panic inside me diminishing with each slap of my hand falling on firm wood.

'You looking for this?' said the brute, and he tossed me my crutch, which landed on my back and rolled off to my side. 'Eggs sunny side up, bacon, and beans.' He pulled out a chair and sat himself down.

I fought the dizziness as best I could, standing up, holding on to the stove for support. My eyes were slow to adjust, and it was but a blur of walls and cupboards and small metal objects and large metal appliances and small oval-shaped pills and small oval-shaped eggs and things that might have been bacon and things that might have been beans that whirled around my line of vision.

'Hurry up in there,' barked the brute. 'How long does it take to fry up some eggs and bacon?'

I don't know how long it took; each second was one of intense concentration just to fight through the dizziness and fight off the nausea. I do not know how I succeeded, but after some time, I staggered back into the living room and dropped a plate of breakfast onto the table for the brute.

'And coffee,' he said. But as I pivoted to return to the kitchen, I collapsed onto the living room floor.

'Never mind. I'll get it myself.'

The light was too bright and the room was spinning too fast for me to keep my eyes open. Instead, I lay on the floor accompanied by jolts of pain emanating from my lower back and shooting down my legs. The pain had a rhythm, a rhythm mimicked by the beat of my heart pounding in my chest, a rhythm disturbed by the sticky mastications of the brute sitting at arm's length behind me.

When I thought I would die, when I hoped I would die, the brute stood from the table. 'That was the worst fucking breakfast I've ever had,' he said, and moments later—or perhaps hours—he left, slamming the front door as he stormed out.

The sound of the door slamming shut woke me into action. I crawled to the sofa, under which I had hid the hammer and assorted screwdrivers. How long would he be out, I did not know. How long would the floorboards be able to contain the slugs? Of that I was equally unable to guess.

I stabbed the screwdriver into what might have been a crack—my eyes, how could I trust my eyes? I hammered and I pried and I loosened a floorboard. Soon I would be upon the slugs!

Alas, the front door opened.

Kneeling on the floor, with my back to the door, I clutched the hammer and focused on summoning strength to my legs should I have to spring and spin and smash the brute's skull to bits.

'What on earth are you doing?' My loyal friend's voice, as worried and pained as it was, came as a relief.

I eased my grip on the hammer. I did not need to turn, for immediately she got on her knees beside me and put a gentle arm around me. 'This again?' she said.

'Yes, this again.' I spoke with such conviction and clarity of mind that there could be no dispute. 'The board is just about to come off. Help me with it, and you will see.'

My loyal friend was much stronger than I, and with her help, we ripped the board from the floor with ease. I did not reel back at the sight there before us. I did not shriek or cover my face in disgust. I had prepared myself; I had imagined the worst.

My loyal friend, on the other hand, let out a gasp and fell back, knocking into the corner table and sending the lamp to crash to the floor. 'My God!'

Though I had my hammer raised, ready to pound, ready to smash the dozens of dormant insects in their nest, I did not deliver any fatal blows. What lay beneath the floorboard was not a nest of larva or slugs, but one plump decaying severed finger.

My loyal friend poked at it with a screwdriver. It moved, though very little, as the skin and muscle at the exposed end had grafted itself to the floor's foundation. 'Oh, my God,' my loyal friend exclaimed again. 'What in the—'

She started to form questions as to how and what and why, but she did not dare complete them.

Though I had expected to find slugs, I was not surprised to find the brute's severed finger rotting away under the floorboard. I was too grounded in reality to expect a simple end to the torments he'd been inflicting on me. He had put it there; he had planned this. From when, I cannot be certain. But he had known, just as I knew at that moment, that he would not leave me alone, not even for a minute. When he was at work in the factory or out drinking in the bars, there was a piece of him back home; a piece true in nature to the whole: a filthy, rotting, stinking vile thing.

I leaned over, picked up my crutch, and pulled myself off the floor. As I walked across the living room, I felt no pain. For the first time in over four months, I walked with no pain! The clarity of my plan, the sureness of my purpose, worked healing powers no medication could rival. My legs were strong, and my back was straight. The crutch in my hand was no longer a thing I gripped for dear life, a thing I clung to for fear I fall. The crutch was my staff, anticipating and announcing my next step.

I entered the kitchen, opened the dishwasher, and pulled out a small Tupperware container. I returned to the exposed burial site and knelt.

'What are you going—' my loyal friend started. But she didn't dare finish the question.

***

My strength, at least some of it, had returned to me, and not a day too soon, for I was forced to call upon it that very evening. The brute returned in a foul mood, fouler than usual. He stank of booze and sweat, and each word he spat out was accompanied with a cloud of toxic vapours that hung thick in the air. He found me sitting—not lying—on the sofa.

'I'm (hic) hungry.' He belched, and paint peeled from the ceiling.

I pinched my nose and sealed my lips tight.

'Did you hear me, woman? (hic) I said I'm (hic) hungry!' His balance waivered, and he reached for the table. I watched him stumble and struggle to keep his head up and was delighted with the show.

'Get in there (hic)'—he pointed with an unsteady hand to the kitchen—'get in there and make me (hic) something to eat.'

He nearly fell again. This time, his foot caught in the floorboard my loyal friend and I had put back, though admittedly not with the clean precision of skilled carpenters. 'What the—' He looked down with confusion as to the irregularity in the floor his eyes were clearly attempting to alert his dull mind to.

To divert his attention, I stood and said, 'Sure, I'll make you something to eat. How does a nice hearty stew sound?'

He looked from the floor to me, though his swaying head and glazed eyes had difficulty adjusting to the sudden change in perspective. He belched. 'And bring me a beer.'

I brought him a beer then returned to the kitchen. Soon after I had begun cooking, the nausea returned, yet stronger than any nausea I had experienced in recent times, accompanied by dizziness and pain. From in front of the stovetop where I was stirring a pot of simmering meats in a thick tomato sauce, I could see the end of the sofa. Oh, how I longed to lie down. *How nice it will be to rest and possibly sleep,* I thought.

But this comforting thought came to me before it rained shards.

'Hurry up (hic) in there!'

The stew bubbled and boiled, the red tomato sauce popping like bloody zits, chunks of meat bobbing up and down like corpses caught in a current. I took a pill or two to fight off the nausea.

'I'm still waiting! (hic) I ain't getting (hic) any younger.'

The scent of my creation filled the kitchen. I opened a window, and howling winds swept in, knocking into the cupboards and rattling any loose furniture or furnishings it could find. I took a pill or two to fight off the dizziness.

The brute banged on the table, reminding my body and my face of his blows. I took a pill or two to fight off the pain.

I ladled out a bowl of stew and carried it to the brute sitting at the table in the living room. My legs trembled, and the room spun around me, but I managed to set the bowl on the table.

'Took you long enough! And you've spilt nearly half of it. Look at the floor!'

I did look at the floor, speckled with drops of red. I fought back the urge to vomit and staggered to the sofa where I collapsed.

'This stew is horrible,' said the brute, but he shovelled in spoonful after spoonful, and he slurped and he chewed and he belched. 'The worst God-damned stew I've ever God-damn eaten.' He loosened his belt and unbuttoned the bottom buttons of his shirt.

His stomach rumbled, and the flabs of his belly shook and jiggled with the activity occurring underneath. The brute stood; one hand clutched the table for support; the other held his belly. 'I don't feel so good.'

He belched again, and red and yellow spittle escaped his mouth and ran down his chin. 'Woman, you trying to poison me!'

I was waging my own war with nausea and could not reply to his accusation. I tried to focus on the ceiling, yet out of the corner of my eye I saw the brute lumber into the kitchen.

'What the hell (hic) did you put in that stew?'

I did not answer, and the question came again.

'You do the shopping,' I said, though far more meekly than I would have liked. 'I put in whatever meats you brought home.'

'I can't get a decent meal!' The brute took the crutch I had left in the kitchen, and he smashed it against the refrigerator. 'Not happy to take off one of my fingers, so you put poison in my food!' He reappeared in the living room, the crutch wielded above his head. 'What do you have to say to that, woman?'

'I'm sorry you didn't like the stew.'

He smashed the ceramic bowl with a blow from the crutch. Shards shot out in all directions. He swung the crutch, sweeping the larger broken bits of the bowl and sending them hurling past my head to the wall behind me. The pieces shattered into dust that sprayed my face with prickling particles.

I closed my eyes and thus could only hear the brute's rampage: my crutch swung and slashed and hitting and smacking and breaking and smashing.

'Oh, my fucking stomach,' he moaned.

I stole a peek and saw him drop the crutch to the floor, grab his belly, and stagger out of the room and down the hall.

The wind had picked up and was currently whipping up pieces of porcelain and shards of wood and sending them whirling about in an imitation of the brute's tantrum. Despite the pain and the dizziness, I pulled myself off the sofa and went to the kitchen to shut the window.

From the kitchen, I had a full view of the living room: like a tornado had passed through it, the desk toppled over, the chair in pieces, the corner table split down the middle, one of its legs severed and lying in splinters clear on the other side of the room. Even my crutch, as sturdy and strong as it had been for me, lay on the floor cracked, with strips of metal peeling off its sides.

I stepped back into the living room to retrieve it, and the floorboards creaked loudly beneath my feet, so loudly that the brute called out from the bedroom, 'Woman!'

I knelt to pick up the crutch and examined the damage to it. As I was peeling off flakes of metal, I heard the brute get out of bed. I hurried to the sofa, hoping I'd make it there before he came into the room.

The brute, however, did not come into the living room. Instead, he went to the bathroom. He left the door open so I could hear him groan and curse and relieve himself loudly.

I focused on salvaging what I could from the crutch. It was a mess: no longer solid enough to support me, no longer robust and imposing as a staff to walk proudly across the room when my body would permit it. The base of it had splintered. Instead of thick and round, the strut was thin and flat; instead of a sturdy blunt tip, it ended in a sharp point. It resembled more a sword than a crutch, and that suited me just as well.

The brute came lumbering down the hallway. He stopped at the threshold, hands on his hips, naked torso jiggling its flabby flesh. 'I ain't never felt worse in all my life.'

He did not have my sympathy.

'And it's all your fault.'

Though I didn't believe him for a second, I was flattered at the thought I could inflict so much suffering on him.

He stepped into the living room, and his plodding feet immediately stumbled over a loosened floorboard. 'What the—' He bent over to examine the floor more closely, then he cast his accusatory eyes on me. 'What in damnation happened to the floor?'

Though the room was still spinning around me and pain was at that moment shooting up my back and down my legs, I pulled myself up and sat facing him. 'Well, look at the mess you've made of this room. You've smashed it to pieces. Are you surprised that the floor was damaged in your tantrum?'

He rose. His eyes widened with indignation.

'What did you expect to happen?' I continued. 'You think you can tear the place apart then find it in pristine condition moments later?'

He stepped toward me. He extended his arm and pointed at me with his stumped finger. 'What I expect,' he said through gritted teeth, 'is to eat a decent meal and not get sick right afterwards.' His mouth twisted into a nauseated scowl, and he put a hand to his belly where the flesh also twisted at his touch.

'And I expect,' he continued, his mangled digit reaching for me, getting nearer and nearer, 'my wife to get off her fat lazy ass once in a while and do some housework.' He stomped his foot, and the loose floorboard rattled.

'I expect,' he continued as he bent down to inspect the floor, 'to be able to walk through my own God-damned living room and not trip over some hazard you've left lying around.' He yanked at the floor board, and I gasped. It came off with ease. He tossed it to the side.

'Some homemaker you are,' he said, and he pried up another board and tossed it to the side. 'This place is a mess. Why don't you do some bloody housework for a change?'

I held my breath, for he was working his way back, back toward the floorboard that had only the day prior concealed his severed digit. Soon he would know that I had discovered his ruse. And I doubted he would take too kindly to that realization.

He tore up a third floorboard then a fourth. Yet as his hand reached down for the infamous one, his stomach shifted and growled. He belched and coughed up a mouthful of red and black liquid which he spat on the ground.

'You did try to poison me, didn't you?' His attention, luckily, was diverted from the floorboards. His attention, unluckily, was directed at me. He approached with his mutilated stump pointing and shaking. 'Admit it, woman! Admit what you've done.'

I shook my head.

'Admit it!'

I clamped down on my lips, for his hand was aimed at my mouth and ever so near.

'This ends here!' he yelled. 'You served me something vile. I'll serve you something vile.' I turned my head, but he thrust that bandaged stump in my face and searched for my mouth.

A roar of a scream was building inside me. And though I felt like a volcano ready to erupt, I concentrated on keeping my lips tightly sealed.

His stump found my nostrils then squirmed in search of my lips. I turned my head, but he grabbed my hair with his other hand and jerked my head back.

The scream escaped. The brute lunged, his stumped hand aiming for my open mouth.

I would like to say that I had planned it all out, that I had calculated move after move like a chess master. But if I'm being honest, it was not careful planning that saved me, but instinct. When he lunged, I pulled the crutch up and jabbed him with it. Any old crutch would have pushed him off of me, would have sent him and his stumped digit away from me. But I did not have any old crutch in my hand; I had a crutch whose strut had been shredded and whose tip sharpened, and the crutch I'd jabbed him with pierced his fat belly.

Oh, the sound of it! Like that of a giant puss-bloated bug stomped on and squished under the heel of a boot.

The tip of the crutch pierced; the edge sliced; and the whole slipped from my hand and landed at my feet. The brute jerked back and tripped over a discarded floorboard. He landed, with spectacular momentum, on his back while several uprooted floorboards fell on top of him.

And then came the slugs.

Amid the debris, I stood looking down at the brute. Mercifully, a floorboard had landed on his face; mercifully, another board had landed on his arm and hid from me his mutilated hand. Only his bloated belly protruded from the wreckage: his bloated yet punctured and slit-open belly. Black bile bubbled out of the gash and trickled down the sides. In its wake, a thick black slug slithered free; behind it, a second smaller slug, then a third, then a dozen more. They oozed from his entrails with blackened blood lubricating their escape like afterbirth.

The brute loosed a low bellowing moan that shook the room, a moan that would have sent shivers down my spine had I not been so overjoyed at the realization that the brute was still alive and, thus, suffering so.

'You were right, my dear,' I said. 'This place *is* a mess. It's time I did some bloody housework for a change.'

The first of the legion of slugs had plopped down from his body onto the floor, and I crushed it with the heel of my shoe, smushing and twisting, reveling in the sound, in the feel, in the sight of black mush squirting out from under my foot.

And they came to me slow and slimy, and one by one I crushed them. The pain in my back subsided in spectacular fashion. I pranced about the room, in a dance one could say, crushing slugs with my light graceful steps. Some of the slugs tried to make their way under the floorboards, but slugs are so slow, and I, with renewed force and renewed mobility, was so quick.

I tried to count them as I crushed them, amazed at the quantity. I stopped counting at thirty-seven—such a glorious number. I'd guess I crushed another thirty-seven thereafter. And I did not tire.

I kicked at the body of the brute when it had ceased spilling out slugs. 'Would you look at me now? My fat lazy ass is finally off the sofa.

Maybe you'd like me to whip you up something to eat.'

In response, his eyes rolled back in his head, his lips parted, and he belched. A fat black slug popped out of his mouth and squeezed its fat slug body out from between his lips. It slid down his cheek, smearing it with black bile, and landed on the floor beside my foot.

'This ends here,' I said, and under the heel of my shoe, I crushed the last of the slugs.

TABLE FOR ONE

It was supposed to be a twenty-four hour stomach flu: the throes of a dying virus waging a final, desperate attempt at growth and reproduction. My body was supposed to be on guard against such an intrusion. It was supposed to be strong, aggressive, and victorious. But I'd always had a low white blood cell count—and with no apparent cause; I'd been checked for cancer, bone marrow disorders, autoimmune disorders, enlarged spleen, shrunken spleen, Chron's disease, infections. It comes down to laziness, really: life is a battle my body refused to fight, a war whose outcome was of no interest to my apathetic immune system.

I must, in the interest of truth and fairness, assume some of the blame for my body's ineffectiveness. Whenever my body was attacked, I'd always pump it full of pharmaceuticals. So why would it bother to mount a serious defence on its own? And without a serious defence, it was constantly under attack. Long tired out from continuously, albeit half-heartedly, staving off infections and battling germs and diseases, my body, once again, put up a pitiful fight.

What was supposed to be a twenty-four hour ordeal, lasted, in fact, six days; six days, 300 mg of acetaminophen, 160 mg of dextromethorphan, and 50 mg of diphenhydramine; 360 mg of oseltamivir, 150 mg of zanamivir, and 100 mg of adamantane, and finally the flu was gone—or most of it. Traces of it—its offspring, if you will—remained: lethargy, nausea, and dizziness; cold sweats, hot flashes, and insomnia. I might have killed the flu (and I do say 'I' killed it and not 'my body' killed it) but in the process, I'd been made vulnerable to other viruses. Every surface I'd come into contact with, the very air I breathed, was ripe with them: viruses that saw in me a hospitable host. And my weak, indifferent body did little to persuade them to look elsewhere.

My body's defences were so poor, I suspected the only thing that managed to kill off such or such virus was another stronger one needing to take its place.

Seasonal, swine, and avian; West Nile, Caribbean, Spanish, Asian, and Middle Eastern—I was visited by each and every one. Despite the crippling fatigue resulting from the come-one, come-all motto of my whorish immune system, I managed to find the strength—caffeine and duloxetine strength—to pull myself out of bed and seek help.

I went to see a man who claimed he was a doctor and who charged me accordingly. He boasted all the necessary letters to his name, had all the necessary diplomas on his wall, and he coloured his words with the necessary Latin.

While flipping through the clutter of papers on his desk, he listened to my story, scratched some words on his prescription pad, tore off a page, and handed it to me. 'There is a flu going around,' he said. 'This should take care of it.'

'But there is something else, doctor. There is more to it than that.'

He paused his shuffling of papers long enough to look up at me. I saw myself reflected in his eyeglasses. I saw a tinier reflection of myself in his pupils. I saw myself smaller and smaller the deeper I looked at him and wondered if this was not the doctor's intent. 'I do not know exactly how I can explain it,' I said. 'There is a profound melancholy, apathy to my body. It doesn't even want to fight back. And when it does, it is merely out of scorn or spite. It's like it doesn't know the difference between me and a vulgar virus. Or it does know, and it just doesn't care.'

He blinked, and the tiny me was crushed only to reappear unharmed.

I looked away, out the window, and my gaze fell upon a cloud that looked remarkably like my kidney.

'You are tired from the flu,' the doctor said. 'It's normal. Take these medicines. You'll be right as rain in no time.'

I looked back at him. He had removed his eyeglasses, and I could no longer see myself. 'Rain would mean my kidney-cloud would condense, turn grey, and explode its contents onto the earth,' I said. 'I fail to see what is right about that.'

The doctor said he knew nothing of kidney-clouds and of explosions. I suspected as much. I suspected there were many things he knew nothing of.

The flu was strong, and she put up a valiant fight. There were times when she completely dominated me. She would commandeer all of my strength and force me to lie in bed with not even enough energy to think or to imagine; I merely was, and I felt. It was a terrifyingly wonderful sensation, as if I had surrendered my mind and existed purely and solely on a biological level. I ceased to be the consequence of my experiences and my memories. I was nothing more than a universe of cells seeking to endure.

After five days of intense biological warfare, I grew disgusted with my body, disappointed in its meagre defences and miserable resistance. I had no other recourse than to cheat, to use the chemical to undermine the natural. And with reluctance and resignation and considerable culpability, once again I capitualted; I took my medicine.

'The flu going around,' as Doctor Right-As-Rain had put it, went around—around my head, around my chest, around my stomach, and around my bowels. For forty days and forty nights she made her rounds; she inhabited me; she grew in me; she gained in strength, and then she was gone. I had killed her.

Do you think my body was grateful? Do you think my body offered my conscience any consolation for the crimes it benefitted from?

Quite the contrary.

Whenever I would reminisce on the flu I had hosted, my jealous body would inflict on me splitting headaches. Whenever guilt would slip into my subconscious, my hypocritical stomach would feed off my remorse. It twisted and tugged at me from inside. It thanked me through a constant state of nausea. It soured my meals and even refused to keep much of the food I gave it.

I cleaned and sterilized my exercise room. I laid the yoga mat in the centre, stripped, and sat myself down upon it, facing east, to have a serious discussion with my body.

'I should have let the flu live. She would have been grateful, unlike you. She would have thrived, and it is obvious to me that you do not want to.'

My body responded through a slight burning sensation in my chest.

I saw more doctors who took more of my money and offered me more of their Roman words. But it was all Greek to me.

Drug dealers and charlatans, that's all they are. And I was a fool to have ever sought their counsel. One doctor went so far as to suggest that it was all in my head and what I needed was a shrink.

What I needed was a cleanse.

First, I started with a cleanse of my mind, emptying it of all the nonsense they'd tried to fill it with. That was easy enough, since I'd had the good sense not to understand most of what they'd told me.

Second, I proceeded with a cleanse of my medicine cabinet, tossing out bottles and vials and tablets, pills and balms and sprays.

Third, I ended with a cleanse of my body: an enima followed by a forty-eight hour fast followed by a sweat-session in the sauna.

I came out of the cleanse anew, and I made a pledge: gone are the days I consult doctors; never again shall I consort with those chemical mongers; never again shall I contribute to their commerce. I will remake my body, of course, but I will do so by seeking out the natural. Henceforth, to stave off a cough in the brittle months, I will take an herbal tea with jasmine honey. For the headaches that come pounding in those stressful nights, I will take bee extract. Just a drop.

I never did return to the chemist's. Perhaps they thought me dead. But the truth was quite the contrary. Never had I been more alive.

I had begun a new life in a new world full of discovery—among those discoveries: holistic boutiques, whole food shops, and, praise the universe, Dmitri's Wellness Parlour.

***

'There's nothing wrong with your body,' Dmitri told me.

'But the doctors?'

'Charlatans.'

'But the medi—'

'Poisons.'

He set his hand against my side.

I know what I felt, and there is nothing in this universe that I am more sure of; my liver did move, as would a magnet, to be nearer to his hand, to be closer to his touch.

'Your body is perfect. You are perfect.' Dmitri wore no eyeglasses, and the reflection of myself I saw in his pupils was not tiny but grand. It shimmered and swam amid swirling greens. It was not crushed but cradled when he blinked. 'There is sadness, no doubt,' he continued. 'But the sadness stems from the fact that you are not at one with your body. There is negativity, aggressive negativity within you, poisoning the harmony.'

'Yes!' I said. 'That is exactly it. I can feel it: aggression and negativity inside me.'

Dmitri closed the shop to be alone, uninterrupted with me. He locked the door and drew the blinds. He laid me down on the reception room's sofa—a sofa draped with cloths made from the most natural of threads. He unbuttoned my shirt. Oh, how I did blush, as my shirt was a vulgar poly blend. He rid me of its confines then went into the back to retrieve two crystal rocks clear with purple and pink stones in the centre. He ran the ragged crystals gently over my navel then along my sides.

'Yes, there is a lot of negativity,' he said.

'Can you feel it, too?'

'I can feel it,' he said. 'The crystals can feel it.'

He then ran magnets over my body, small egg-shaped magnets that hovered centimetres above me. I could feel their pull. I could feel the negative toxins within me leave.

'Thank you, Dmitri.'

***

On my second visit to Dmitri's Wellness Parlour, I received glorious news: my Root Chakra was strong. One manifestation of this was a healthy 'earthly' foundation. This was true—just as everything Dimitri told me was true. I had a good job, one I was good at and actually enjoyed doing: purchasing manager for a well-known hotel chain. I had the uncanny ability to make, save, spend, and invest money. I had no financial or material worries. I had a strong 'earthly' foundation upon which a spiritual castle could be built.

My Intuitive Chakra was strong, as well. I knew things without knowing exactly how I knew them or even that I knew them. I did not need to understand all the details or implications of a decision—not on a cognitive level at least—I simply felt and was guided by my feelings.

There were things, of course, that I would need to work on—my Foot Chakra and Sacral Chakra were on top of the list—but Dmitri could help me; Dmitri would help me. And with my strong Root Chakra and strong Intuitive Chakra, I was destined for success and well being.

On my third visit to Dmitri's Wellness Parlour, Dmitri helped me realign my chi. (Oh, how my chi was a twisted and distorted mess.) He placed magnets on various parts of my body and adjusted them slowly so as to facilitate the flow of various energies and auras. There was much resistance from my body, and I was sad.

'Do not worry, my friend,' he said to me. 'You must be patient.'

I smiled, though it was a meek smile and not one that could fool Dmitri.

'You are patient, aren't you?'

'I am,' I said. 'Or at least I will learn to be.'

Through Dmitri I learned of my chi and my Seven Chakras. I learned of nature's vibrations and of my own. I was embarrassed at how ignorant I was of such important things, but Dmitri made no condemnation. He implored me to feel no shame. With Dmitri I was asked to feel no embarrassment. That, as well, I would need to learn.

Through Dmitri, I learned of nature's herbs, roots, and extracts: what they did for the body, naturally, not chemically. I was embarrassed at the quantity of chemicals I had been poisoning myself with: additives, preservatives, sodium nitrate, sodium benzoate, disodium inosinate, monosodium glutonate—not to mention the glucose and the gluten. I hated myself for it, but Dmitri did not judge me. He cared for me and guided me.

And I was getting well. My digestion and my bowels were testament to the harmony Dmitri was restoring in me. Soon I would be whole. I knew that. Though, oh how impatient I was. And, conversely, oh how patient Dimitri was, putting up with my seemingly endless stream of questions and concerns.

'I have been drinking chamomile tea to help me sleep, but it hasn't been working,' I told him.

'Have you been having trouble sleeping, my friend?'

'My body is well, but I am anxious.'

'You feel as though there should be more?'

I nodded.

'You know there is more; there has to be. And you are restless for that 'more', restless to know it and to experience it.'

I nodded emphatically. Dmitri knew me. Dmitri understood me.

'I understand your eagerness,' he said, and he smiled and touched me on the cheek.

***

Since I had rid my home of pill bottles, vaporizers, sprays, and other 'medicines', my once over-stuffed medicine cabinet and cluttered bathroom shelves were now liberated and my home's life force could flow more freely. I improved on this further by throwing out a small desk I hardly used from the living room and hanging a mirror in the hallway. I placed a few crystals around the house, a wind chime at the front door, and a whirligig at the back, thus helping align the vibrations of my home with its life force. I felt the difference immediately. My own vibrations were also better aligned. I, too, became liberated, and the life force in me, too, flowed more freely.

I went to Dmitri's parlour twice a month. I would have gone more often if my budget allowed, but twice a month he would straighten the aura of my body from the outside with magnets and crystals, and he would cleanse my body of toxins from the inside with teas and coffee enemas.

'How are you feeling, my friend?'

'Pure and whole and at peace.'

'Are you happy?'

I sat up from the massage table and looked at him, perplexed. *Am I happy? What ambition is this?* 'I've never considered that question before,' I told him. 'Or at least not since I was a young child.'

Dmitri nodded, for he had expected such an answer.

'It has never really been a concern of mine, nor has it ever been my ambition.'

'Of course not,' he replied.

Did I pass the test? Did he really think me so shallow as to preoccupy myself with questions of my own happiness? Had I succeeded in convincing him of the contrary?

'I seek oneness and harmony. I am willing to accept happiness as a by-product, but I do not seek it.'

Dmitri put his hands on my face. He ran his fingers lightly over my eyes, guiding their lids shut so that I may see darkness, so that I may gaze into the depths of nothingness. His fingertips glided down my neck, over my shoulders, then back up to the top of my cheek bones. I opened myself to his energy. It entered me, filled me, and conversed with my own. It shared with me beauteous words not even thoughts could express. He ran his fingers up to my temples and pressed lightly. His energy shot through my mind. It cradled me in a warm wool blanket, rocked me, and set a finger on my lips. 'Shh.'

I said nothing. My mind slept in comfort.

'At night when you are lying in your bed,' he whispered. 'You will feel your body slowly evaporating, becoming lighter and lighter with each passing moment. You will be pulled, like a wisp of vapour, toward the vacuum of subconsciousness. You will sleep, and you will be revived.' He ended his melodious instructions with a light touch on my eyelids. They opened, and I saw Dmitri's face, confident and serene.

***

Since I met Dmitri, my body underwent a drastic change. My chakras were strengthened. My chi was aligned and flowing better—though with so many negative vibrations around me, at work and in my commute, it was constantly being dampened and disrupted. My mind and spirit were opened to new harmonies, universal harmonies that before I had not even been aware of.

Since I met Dmitri, my diet, as well, went through a radical revolution. Gone were the trans fats and saturated fats, the pesticides and herbicides, the chemical preserves and additives, the GMOs, HMOs, and IMOs. I ate, instead, holistically: the fresh and the natural; whole grains and raw or minimally processed foods; the organically grown fruits and vegetables of Dmitri's garden.

For the first time in years, my body relaxed its revolt. Instead of feeling heavy and sluggish, I was light and vivacious. Instead of my thoughts tied to aches and pains, my thoughts were free to explore, investigate, and contemplate. Light and vivacious, investigate and contemplate—concepts and words that before had been mysterious and complex became truths, evident and simple. I began to see the universe, to understand it, not with my eyes, not with my mind, but with the entirety of my biology. Whereas I once was but a babe suckling from a poisonous teat, now weaned, I was presently free to grow—biologically and spiritually, if ever there were a difference.

'I had no idea there was so much flavour in a simple bell pepper,' I told Dmitri, partly because it was true but also to thank him and congratulate him on such a successful harvest. Dmitri, of course, was an expert gardener. He was in touch, no, in tune with nature, and it yielded for him generously and harmoniously.

'Nature is a beautiful thing,' he responded, 'when we don't adulter it with poisons and pesticides.'

He showed me his garden, which was much smaller than I had imagined. But Dmitri was an expert at making the most of the space. Though the plants appeared to be cramped, upon closer inspection, I could see that each grew without a bent stem or crinkled leaf. Even in close confines they all lived and grew together like symbiotic organisms feeding one another, feeding off one another: an ecological food chain where there was neither predator nor prey, only peace and prosperity.

'It's beautiful, don't you think?'

He was proud of his garden. And why wouldn't he be? I was proud of him, yet ashamed of myself, ashamed that my own garden, while nearly twice the size, bore only the fruit of neglect.

'Why are you sad? What's troubling you?'

'Oh, Dmitri.' I covered my disgraceful face. 'My garden is little more than a few flowers, and even they are reluctant to show their petals.'

He took my hand from my eyes and gently placed it at my side. 'Don't be so hard on yourself. It takes a lot of time to cultivate a garden, a lot of time and know-how.'

'Will you teach me?'

He smiled. 'Of course, I will teach you.'

In his parlour, he sold packets of seeds and bulbs bought from noble farmers. And though I selected many I thought would be great in my garden, he simply shook his head. He got on one knee, and with no tool but his fingers and nails, he snipped for me bulbs he himself had cultivated. He collected seeds from his fruits and roots from his vegetables.

'Dmitri, you are too kind. How will I ever repay you?'

He touched me on my belly and on my forehead. 'Your wellness is thanks enough.'

***

In fewer than ten months my vibrations became more in tune with Dmitri's. When we were near each other, there was no discord. There was clarity, and there was peace.

When we were apart—though I carried with me at all times a collection of red stones he'd given me (red stones are especially good at retaining positive vibrations)—I felt disconnected. Of course there was still peace, however, a fainter, more distant peace. And in place of clarity, there was longing.

I knew Dmitri felt it as well—I had, after all, a strong Intuitive

Chakra. I began to collect rubies, garnets, and carnelians. I would sleep with them so that they'd retain my vibrations. Then I'd give them to him to hold onto until we could be together again. Oh, if not for the demands of my job! If not for the demands of his!

To appease this longing between sessions, I spent more and more time in my garden with Dmitri's seeds and Dmitri's bulbs and Dmitri's roots. I planted. I culled. I fertilized, and I sowed. My efforts were rewarded with a vast, bustling garden that yielded its life selflessly to mine. With the exception of the oils and the grains I purchased from Dmitri, I ate only what I grew myself. I had true domain over my body, and with it came a calmness of spirit. Like the triangle Dimitri would trace on my forehead with the light touch of his anointed finger, I had formed a perfectly symetrical union of the three: spirit, body, and nature.

I shared with Dmitri—just as he did with me—my newfound joy. He was happy for me. Of course he was. Though, as he ran crystals over my body, I could see concern in his eyes.

'What is it, Dmitri? I eat now only of the plants I cultivate myself. Have I not expunged the toxins from my body? Am I not pure and at one with nature?'

'Of course you are pure,' he answered. 'I am, however, concerned about the loss of weight.'

'I will eat more,' I said.

'You promise me?'

'I promise you.'

Not only did I eat more—and only from what I grew myself—but, as Dmitri instructed, I began to give back to the garden, to give of myself. Instead of store-bought fertilizers, I used my own excrement— 'biosolids' he called it. Thus I nourished myself from the garden, and it nourished itself from me. Just as Dmitri did. Just as it should be: the circle of life, a pure and perfect ecological chain. When I ate of my garden, I was, in a way, eating of me. And when I ate of Dmitri's produce, in a way, I was eating of him. That was a beautiful thing. Even more beautiful was the thought, the realization, that Dmitri, as well, was doing the same. Dmitri, in a way, was eating of himself. And Dmitri, in a way, was eating of me. The ecological chain, our ecological chain, was strong and pure and harmonious.

With this realization, my appetite increased tenfold. Dmitri ran crystals along my meat-covered bones, and he was happy. And I was happy.

'You are looking well, my friend,' he said.

'And I feel well,' I replied.

And my garden flourished. And Dmitri's garden flourished. Our ecological chain was strong.

Not only did I gain a few pounds, but the generous yield of my garden meant that I always had food left over to share with Dmitri—at first, soups and veloutés, then with the flour and eggs he'd give me, pies and tarts and quiches.

'Thank you for the eggs, Dmitri.' I handed him a leek and mushroom quiche.

'And thank you for the quiche. You are a spectacular cook, you know?'

I blushed.

'No, really. I don't tell you that enough.' He touched me on the side, and I nearly fell over from the power of his chi. 'You are extraordinary. You truly have a remarkable gift.'

'It is such a pleasure to give,' I said.

This made Dmitri's bright smile brighten even more. 'Isn't it?' he said, and he gave me a box the size of a loaf of bread.

'What is it?'

'It is a gift. Though I'm not quite as competent in the kitchen as you are, I baked these for you.'

Cookies with cranberries, brownies with nuts—I never used to have a sweet tooth, but with Dmitri and his gifts, my palate was expanding, and it did make him so happy to see me eat.

'You're going to make me fat,' I said.

His countenance was severe then quickly lightened. 'Nonsense. You are looking healthier. There is colour in your flesh and meat on your bones. I am happy.'

'Me too, Dmitri. I am happy, oh, so very happy.'

***

If absence makes the heart grow fonder, then what does it do to our vibrations? What does it do to our chi? To our spirit and to our soul? Waiting two weeks to see Dmitri was such a trial. I ate the marinated aubergine he had given me. Waiting two weeks to see Dmitri was such tribulation. I ate the quinoa with pomegranates he had cooked for me.

My body was satisfied. Of course it was. Yet it knew there was greater still. It had felt, it had experienced the purest, the most natural of harmonies, and anything less than that became increasingly difficult to bear. My body would get anxious between our sessions, and the herbal teas were beginning to lose their calming effect. And despite the drops of basswood honey I'd take at night, sleep was becoming more and more difficult to find.

Dmitri was such a generous man and there were so many people besides me that needed him, I had to fight off my selfish urges, fight off the impulse to stop by the parlour after work when I hadn't made an appointment. Fortunately, my meagre income would allow me no more than two sessions a month—'fortunately', for I fear, had I the resources, there would be a great number of needy bodies that would be deprived of his council. Were I wealthy, I would book one session a day—no two: a crystal bath in the morning, a magnet cleanse in the afternoon, and a coffee enema on Fridays!

I had to exercise a bit of restraint: one crystal bath in the middle of the month and one magnet cleanse at the end of the month. No more. And I forced myself to stop by the parlour with a gift only once or twice a week. For when I did, it was inevitable that we would converse, we would commune, and his other clients would have to wait. And though my Root Chakra was strong, it was inevitable that I'd buy some organic oils or Swiss chards or beets whenever I'd stop buy. And though he tried on many occasions to gift me with radishes or potatoes or pumpkin, I had to insist on paying. Dmitri was too generous, and I would not take advantage of him.

***

'How are you feeling, my friend?' Dmitri asked as he laid me down on the massage table.

I closed my eyes. 'I am well. Very well.'

'I am glad.' He touched me lightly in the strategic points where my chi was tangled. 'And how is your body?'

'I am well. Very well.'

'That wasn't my question.'

I opened my eyes, and he shut them again with a suggestion. He did not run the crystals over my body as usual. Instead, he arranged them, creating an outline around me.

'What are you—'

'Shh,' he said. 'We must listen to your body. *You* must listen to your body.'

He had me shut my eyes.

I listened, though my body's demands were confused.

Dmitri lit a lavender-scented candle and applied a touch of olive oil to my forehead.

I listened more carefully, and my body spoke with more clarity.

'I think it wants—'

'Shh.' He placed a finger delicately on my lips. 'You must listen only.'

He applied oil to my neck. I recognized the oil as that in which he marinated the aubergines, and my body spoke with unequivocal clarity, shouting almost, yearning and pleading.

When we finished, I began to speak of what my body had told me, but Dmitri silenced me again. He shook his head. 'Between us, we need not words. I can hear you perfectly, just as you can hear your body perfectly.'

'Now, I can,' I replied. 'Thank you, Dmitri.'

He shook his head once more. 'No, it is I who thank you.'

***

On my next visit to Dmitri's Wellness Parlour, I received glorious news. 'I would like to see you every week,' Dmitri said.

'I cannot afford that,' I said, but he put his index finger over my mouth and shook his head.

'Please, this is not about money. You and my other clients are giving me enough to keep the palour open and to share the message of true healing. No, I want to see you every week, but I don't want more money than you are already giving me.'

How could I refuse him? Why would I refuse him?

'And please,' he said, 'do stop by more often; I so enjoy baking for you. Will you do that? Will you stop by more often between sessions so that I may share more with you?'

How could I refuse him? Why would I refuse him?

I am not a fool. It is harmony I seek, and through Dmitri, I am harmonious. We are harmonious. *Why not every day, Dmitri?* Though I lacked the courage to say those words aloud, I implored them to the surface of my eyes. I implored them to permeate the energy I was sending him. 'We will see each other every week,' I said. 'And I will stop by more often.'

'I am glad,' he replied.

'I am glad,' I replied.

I did not pay him extra, as he had so humbly insisted, though he could not stop me from buying more culinary aids from his shop—after all, he was giving me cakes and quinoa and pastas and pies, and he refused to allow me to pay full price. I continued to cook, even more so, for I was not cooking for merely my body alone but also for his. I would come to his parlour every Monday and Tuesday with a homemade dish. Soon thereafter, I would come to his parlour on Thursdays, as well, and on whatever day I knew Dmitri would want a tart or a quiche.

He would close the shop early whenever I came by. We would eat together, in the back, in the room reserved for healing. He would fold up the massage table and replace it with three blocks of wood in the guise of a table. We would sit on cushions laid on the carpet, crossed-legged, across from each other, his body, his movements a mirror of mine. When he ate, I would take but a symbolic bite merely to accompany him. I nourished myself by watching him eat. Through Dmitri being fed, I, too, was fed.

'It's delicious. Thank you.'

I shook my head. 'It is I who thank you.'

***

At first, I suspected my body was becoming jealous of Dmitri, as it refused to let me sleep and dream of him. Instead, it began troubling my nights with gastric torments and often sharp pains in the heart. But it loved pies made from the gluten-free flour Dmitri would provide me, and my body loved digesting them in his presence. In fact, it would properly digest only the foods I ate in his presence. It was I who should have been jealous. But I was not petty, not like my body, and I was not jealous, not in the least. I was happy: happy that my body was happy, and happy that Dmitri was as well.

Despite the troubled nights, I continued to radiate positive energy which, in turn, came back to me in the most delightful of details. I craved—oddly enough—onions, and my garden happened to offer me onions of a perfect roundness. My body begged for aubergine, and though it was well in advance of harvesting season for aubergine, my garden yielded aubergines of a deep and inviting purple.

The universe and I were at one. The message was clear, and I heeded it without delay. I united the necessary ingredients, took the day off from work, and devoted the afternoon to making him—making us— an aubergine and onion pie. I was filled with joy and with wellness imagining Dmitri's peaceful countenance as he ate what I was preparing. I kneaded the dough and cut the vegetables, but my capricious concentration refused to stay still, how eager I was to finish and bring him the pie and watch him partake.

As I lined the pan with the dough, my thumb scraped along the edge, tearing skin and breaking a vein. I jerked my hand away, lest a drop of blood contaminate the pie. With my acute vision—bestowed upon me through months of taking carotene supplements—I did spy a tiny flake of skin stuck to the edge of the pan. I did not wipe it off. Instead, I flicked it onto the dough. *It is so tiny, he will never notice.*

I then imagined Dmitri digesting the pie, savouring the pie, digesting a small part of me, savouring a small part of me. How delicious I was to him. How nourishing and satisfying.

I revelled in this glorious fantasy; I would have stayed, as such, enraptured, but reality beckoned and I eventually came to my senses. *Do I seek to hide from Dmitri? How lesser is the joy if he does not notice, if he cannot share in the true spirit of the act? Do I not give him these dishes because I want to share?*

I held my hand above the pan. I took the carrot grater and rubbed it against my wounded thumb. The pain was intense. It sent my mind fleeing, and I forgot how to feel. I remembered only how to peel, and I did manage to peel off quite a substantial sliver of skin. So much so, that I deemed it best to take scissors and cut the slice into smaller pieces. More than a few drops of blood were added to the mix. I then bandaged my thumb and re-kneaded the dough with its added ingredients.

***

'What happened to your thumb?' asked Dmitri, nodding to my bandaged appendage.

'I had a little accident while preparing this pie.' I handed him my offering. He took it and smiled.

'Thank you. I will honour your sacrifice.'

'I am honoured, but I want you to enjoy it, as well,' I said.

'And I will enjoy it, thoroughly,' he said. And I knew it was true. 'Please sit.' He motioned to the massage table which had been lowered. He had draped on it a silk cloth and had set two plates, two sets of cutlery, and two cups for tea. Two cylindrical cushions lay on either side.

'The table reserved for healing,' I said, 'how appropriate.'

He took my hand and was my equilibrium as I lowered myself onto the cushion. 'Let us heal,' he said, and he took a seat opposite me.

I watched him cut the pie into two large, perfectly symmetrical parts. Then he cut those two parts into four equal parts. He scooped one up and extended it toward my plate.

'None for me, thanks.'

'Oh?' he responded with a tilt of the head and a lift of the brow. His eyes darted from my lips to my bandaged thumb then back. 'And why, pray tell, might that be?'

He was playing with me, and I was overjoyed. A smile stretched across my blushing face. 'This is the kind of pie that one makes solely for the giving,' I responded.

'I see,' said Dmitri. 'The ultimate sacrifice. But it is still a dish we can share.' He sliced the piece of pie with the side of his fork. Then with a gentle and precise poke, Dmitri picked up one of the halves by the tip of the fork's prongs. 'You did prepare this for us to share, right?'

I nodded. 'I prepared it for us to share.'

'Thank you,' he said, and he placed the bite in his mouth.

As I watched the morsel slide down his throat, a chill ran down my spine. My arms twitched, and I felt a warm touch on the base of my back.

'It's good, don't you think?' he asked.

I opened my mouth to speak, but then I chose to answer him with my mind. *It is good. It feels so right.*

Dmitri kept his eyes locked on mine as he served himself a second slice. This time he chewed it slowly, letting it mull around in his mouth, savouring it, letting me savour it.

I ate nothing that night, but I hungered not. I felt a glorious sensation under the bandages of my thumb: a burning, a throbbing, like a pulse of pure pleasure.

I returned three days later with a salmon and spinach quiche. Dmitri kissed the bandaged stubs of my index and middle finger, took my hand, and led me to the back for our lunch. I drank a tea for natural and holistic healing and watched Dmitri enjoy my offering.

I ate nothing that night, but I hungered not. I slept—though a somewhat troubled sleep—with dreams of cells uniting; from many they became one; from disorder came clarity and purpose.

I returned three days later with malfatti in red sauce. Dmitri ran crystals over my bandaged forearm and gave me juniper leaves and comfrey root to ensure a quick and thorough healing. He, then, took my hand and led me to the back for our lunch. I was hungry, and I did feast on the sight of Dmitri enjoying the spinach and ricotta dumplings.

I ate nothing that night, but I hungered not. My subconscious summoned me. It shared with me colours and shapes, patterns my conscious mind would only cloud with reason. It was beautiful, but alas, it was fleeting.

I awoke alone in my own bed, alone in my own body. Though my stubbed fingers did throb, and the abrasions on my arm did burn, I was not sick. I was sad yet could not find the cause. I felt empty but heavy at the same time. My mind understood that my body needed to see Dmitri, but it failed to find the force to lift me out of the sheets. I lay there lamenting my emptiness, lamenting more than ever my biology.

I lay there until I was visited by hunger. We lay together, then hunger grew tired and bored and left.

The following evening, a beep from my phone informed me that I had received a text message. Suspecting it was from Dmitri, I found the force to crawl across the bed to the nightstand to retrieve my phone. 'I'm getting hungry,' it read.

I fell back onto the bed, clutching the phone to my heart. The corners of my mouth stretched until I thought they would snap.

Despite having slept all day, I was too tired but to lie there and smile and dream.

I sent Dmitri a text message saying as much and prayed him to set the table for the following evening.

I was so excited I put extra thyme in my chamomile tea.

That night, at midnight, when I closed my eyes and felt my body dissipating like vapour, it was not a vacuum sucking me in. It was a tongue; it was peristalsis. It was Dmitri.

I slept until the following evening. I awoke, excited about my gift, yet incredibly nervous and agitated for a reason I could not understand.

I arrived at Dmitri's shortly after closing.

Dmitri welcomed me with a kiss on both cheeks. He touched my hand and my agitation was lifted. 'Come.' He led me through the beaded curtain and into the back of his parlour. The massage table lay against the wall. In its place was a larger wooden table, more suitable for dining. There were two wicker chairs placed on either side, two large obelisk crystals, and one plate, one knife, and one fork. A few candles on the floor offered their flames and filled the room with a light scent of lavender.

Dmitri pulled out the chair for me. 'Take a seat,' he said.

I did as he instructed.

He sat opposite me and placed his hands on the crystals. A peaceful smile spread across his lips. 'Touch,' he said. 'Place your hands on the crystals next to mine.'

I did as he instructed.

'There. Can you feel that?'

And I could feel it. It was beauteous, harmonious. It was hot and cold. It was rough and smooth. It was Dmitri's energy. It was mine. It was ours.

Dmitri lifted his hands from the crystals and touched me on the back of my wrists as he got up. 'I've prepared you a tea.'

He left the room and returned shortly with a porcelain teacup and saucer and a silver tea service. He set the cup before me and poured. 'This tea will free you from the instructions of your nerves. They will have no more control over you and what you feel. You, and you alone, will choose what you want to do and what you want to feel.'

The aroma coming from the cup was bitter, and it stung my nose. I winced. Dmitri laughed. 'It tastes better once it goes down.' He set the tea service on the floor behind him, stood before me, and watched as I picked up the cup and brought it to my lips. He watched as I drank and smiled as I winced again at the bitter taste. 'How do you feel?' he asked.

The warm tea flowed down my throat and hit my belly. A wave of calm washed through me. It ran down my legs. My muscles were freed from the tensions binding them together. My whole body was fleeing its confines, and I had but the strength to grip the table, lest I slide into a puddle of myself on the floor. I answered him with a giddy grin.

Dmitri slowly unbuttoned my shirt. I cursed myself for not having worn a pullover so that he may rid me of it much faster. Yet I was patient as he undid every last button. I was patient as he slipped the shirt off me. And I was patient as he folded it and set it on the floor.

I tried to stand, but my legs were dreaming and could not be woken. I teetered and nearly fell.

Dmitri took my hands and steadied me. I fixed his eyes with mine. His stare strengthened me, summoned me, and lifted me toward him. He pulled me up and sat me on the table. I leaned my body against his. I no longer felt my body, not my own; I felt his. I felt ours.

I did not feel alone.

I felt his chi flow with mine, flow as ours.

I did not feel the air separating us.

I felt his vibrations marry with my mine and vibrate as ours.

I did not feel the knife touch my side.

I looked down to watch Dmitri carefully and expertly carve out a strip. With his other hand he touched my chin and lifted my gaze back up to his. He opened his mouth, and I could see, down his throat, a welcoming glow flicker against the muscles of his oesophagus. I watched him place the meat in his mouth. Drops of blood disappeared on his tongue. The meat bathed in saliva. His mouth closed around it, and I was wrapped in a warm and gentle euphoria.

About The Author

Born in Paris, France, Michaël Wertenberg moved to the US as a young child where he cultivated his passion for books, notably with the works of Edgar Allen Poe and Clive Barker. It was, however, his passion for music that he would follow initially. This led him to Nashville, Tennessee. There he cut his teeth as a guitarist in recording studios playing on sessions for pop and crossover artists before moving to New York to explore the city's vibrant jazz scene.

He would return to his native Paris and shift his focus away from the guitar and on to orchestral composition. While working on an opera, Buck v. Bell, the constant inward examination - imagining harmonies and rhythms and trying to transcribe them onto paper - eventually provoked a severe case of hyperacusis - an extreme, often painful, sensitivity to sound.

He was forced to give up his musical pursuits and seek out another means of creative expression - one that would also provide him with the silence he so desperately needed. It was then that he turned to his first love, literature.

He frequently works as a ghostwriter on erotica and romance series, while his own work tends to focus on aberrations of the mind, especially in regard to our fascinating yet frightening ability to rationalize the irrational. His short stories have been published in numerous literary reviews and genre anthologies and have since been compiled into single-author collections.

He left Paris, France in 2014 and has since been moving from country to country around Europe looking for somewhere to call home. He currently resides in Budapest, Hungary with his cat, Zvyezda, where he conducts the occasional writing workshop and puts on the occasional one-man comedy show.

Also by
Michaël Wertenberg

THE ORTHOGRAPHY OF MADNESS AND MISGIVINGS

A compilation of his short fiction (previously published in literary reviews and genre anthologies as well as some previously unpublished pieces) – The collection spans three years and five countries, and the stories are organized according to the country he was living in at the time of their creation. Short biographical passages introduce each country section, giving insight into the writer's mindset at the time, his motivation for moving, and his experience in the new country.

The collection contains literary fiction, horror, humour, and the surreal, but it could also be considered 'travel log fiction', if that's a thing.

STORIES TO TELL YOUR CHILDREN
(assuming you are a very bad parent)

A collection of six modern horror fables – a monster with a taste for disobedient boys; conflicting superstitions that conspire to the same dark end; a Thanksgiving massacre with all the fixings; a touching Christmas celebration (with cleaver and shackle line!); mutating siblings; and a new twist on an old classic.

Running Wild Press publishes stories that cross genres with great stories and writing. RIZE publishes great genre stories written by people of color and by authors who identify with other marginalized groups. Our team consists of:

Lisa Diane Kastner, Founder and Executive Editor
Mona Bethke, Acquisitions Editor, Editor, RIZE
Benjamin White, Acquisitions Editor, Editor, Running Wild Press
Peter A. Wright, Acquisitions Editor, Editor, Running Wild Press
Rebecca Dimyan, Editor
Andrew DiPrinzio, Editor
Cecilia Kennedy, Editor
Barbara Lockwood, Editor
Cody Sisco, Editor
Chih Wang, Editor
Pulp Art Studios, Cover Design
Standout Books, Interior Design
Polgarus Studios, Interior Design
Nicole Tiskus, Production Manager
Alex Riklin, Production Manager
Alexis August, Production Manager

Learn more about us and our stories at www.runningwildpress.com

Loved these stories and want more? Follow us at www.runningwildpress.com, www.facebook.com/runningwildpress, on Twitter @lisadkastner @RunWildBooks @RwpRIZE